# HISTORY
# OF COLD
# SEASONS

*Also by Joshua Harmon*

QUINNEHTUKQUT

SCAPE

LE SPLEEN DE POUGHKEEPSIE

THE ANNOTATED MIXTAPE

# HISTORY
# OF COLD
# SEASONS

JOSHUA HARMON

DZANC
BOOKS

Dzanc Books
5220 Dexter Ann Arbor Road
Ann Arbor, MI 48103
dzancbooks.org

ISBN 978-1-936873-43-2
Cover design by Steven Seighman
Cover photograph by Andrew Zawacki

Grateful acknowledgment is made to the publications in which these stories were originally published, sometimes in slightly different form:

*American Letters & Commentary:* "Sundowning"
*Antioch Review:* "The Burning House," "The Lighthouse Keeper"
*Black Warrior Review:* "The Fisherman and His Wife"
*BOMB:* "The Dead Man"
*Chelsea:* "History of Cold Seasons"
*Massachusetts Review:* "Dundee"
*New England Review:* "The Passion of Asa Fitch"
*TriQuarterly:* "Rope"
*Verse:* "Dear Oklahoma"
*Witness:* "Hattie Dalton," "Signs"

Library of Congress Cataloging-in-Publication Data

Harmon, Joshua, 1971–
[Short stories. Selections]
History of cold seasons / Joshua Harmon. — First edition.
pages ; cm
ISBN 978-1-936873-43-2 (pbk.)
I. Harmon, Joshua, 1971– Burning House. II. Title.
PS3608.A7485A6 2014
813'.6—dc23
2014037077

Printed in the United States of America

FIRST EDITION

TO MY MOTHER & FATHER

# CONTENTS

The number of creatures that kept a Rigid Fast, shutt up in Snow for diverse weeks together, and were found alive after all, have yielded surprizing stories unto us.

—Cotton Mather,
"A Dreadful Snow Storm"

# HISTORY
# OF COLD
# SEASONS

# ROPE

Our brother keeps a girl tied to a tree in the woods. Mindy and I believe that Jamie, our brother, stole the rope from Joe Letourneau's father's garage, where everyone has seen the stacked coils of it beside the broken-toothed rakes and broken-spoked bikes and broken plastic bits of last Christmas's toys that Mr. Letourneau saves there, or that Jamie doesn't even use a rope—too rough and raspy on his girl's skin—but clotheslines that for months he has at night collected from the backs of houses, using his knife to snick off a length here, a few loops there, or that Jamie has simply snitched the clotheslines new and tight-wound from the wicker basket we once saw them in at the hardware store where our mother had gone for a new lock to put on the door, after one of the men our mother had brought home had left, keeping the copy of the extra key our mother had, a few weeks earlier, sent us to the hardware store to have cut.

At supper we catch our brother sneaking food into his pockets. Later, when he's supposed to be doing his homework at the yard sale desk in his room, we know that he's bellying over his windowsill, slipping down through the branches of the maple there, to bring the food to the girl he keeps tied up in the woods. We know that what our mother or our grandmother might think only a wind-bothered branch bumping against the house is our brother's foot finding a hold, his knee knocking a clapboard. We have seen him swipe the hairbrush from our mother's nightstand, carry it into the bathroom, and, with hair shiny and tucked behind his ears, replace it in her room. When it rains, he steals an umbrella from the closet and sits in the woods with the tied-up girl, holding the umbrella over her head to keep her from getting wet. We believe he also holds her hand. We have guessed he may read to her from a book, sometimes—these days there seems always to be some silent word he is testing out on his lips. Mindy thinks he gives his girl cigarettes pinched from our mother's and grandmother's purses to smoke while she waits for him to come to the woods after school and put her hand in his.

"How can she smoke if her hands are tied up?" is what I wanted to know. "How can she hold hands?"

"Do you think he holds the cigarette up to her lips?" I also wanted to know.

"How can he hold the cigarette, the umbrella, and her hand all at once?" I did not even bother to ask.

❄

"Wake up, wake up, sleepies, wake up," our mother says, and we wake to warmth—first me, then Mindy, yawning and rubbing her eyes—to the smell of smoke beyond the blankets from a fire already filling the woodstove. The smoke smells too smoky, like the fire didn't catch at first, paper blazing blackly away to ashes before it could spark sticks, wood scorched but not burning, until someone added more paper and kindling and kneeled on cold stones to blow embers into flames.

Still, under these bunched and rumpled blankets is the most warmth, and under them we stay—my legs, Mindy's, a breath, a wrinkle, a cool edge by my hand, a kick to free a foot from a tangle of fabric. I can hear the reel of rain on the roof. Through a barely opened eye I see our mother's dark face over my face in bed, her dark hair hanging darkly down to frame it, her robe a loose knot. "Wake up, wake up," she says, almost singing the words. Mindy turns away, and the blankets make a sound that says hush, hush.

Our mother plucks at those blankets and tugs a corner free. The smoke smell is fainter now. What little of the day I can see through an eye half-opened and shut, opened again and shut again, invents itself in blue clouds and rain beyond our drop-streaked window. A Saturday should always be a sleeping day.

But our mother yanks the blankets away, her hands gathering up all the heavy covers and sweeping them into a heap on the floor. There is a sticky taste on my tongue. There is Mindy's scrunched-up foot, and Mindy's half-asleep whine at the lack of a covering. There is someone's eyelash stuck on the pilled pillowcase. Then there is our mother.

"Wake up," our mother says, looking from me to Mindy. "Wake up. You need to find your brother."

Our mother found Miles not long after the Fourth of July, early one evening as the crickets rubbed their legs in the wild weedy grass behind the house. Our mother came home in a loud pickup truck we did not remember seeing, loud enough that until the man driving it turned off the engine we couldn't hear the crickets. She came home with summer's first paper bag of corn for us to shuck the husks and silk from, which she set on the front porch between the two slack-wove folding chairs, with a six-pack of brown bottles that clinked when she carried them into the kitchen to find the churchkey for, and with Miles, who creaked shut the door of his pickup truck, walked up the porch's two sagging steps, and held open the screen door for us, a stub of cigarette in his mouth and his sleeves rolled up to show greeny ink under his skin that might've shaped a face or a flag or a flower, or that maybe might've said someone's name.

"Hey," he said to us, nodding once beneath the grease-fingered brim of his cap. Fireflies winked in the dusky yard behind him. "Corn's on the porch."

"You're letting in the bugs," Mindy said.

Miles had nine and a half fingers and a ponytail and pants that never fit his hips. "Ask him" was what our mother told us to do, and "Don't ask" was what he told us, jacking up those pants and correcting the curl of his cap brim, when we asked him what had happened to the rest of his finger, but then one side of his mouth would pull back and he'd poke us with the smooth-skinned end

4

of that stump until we ran away. That stump, the end of it, had a seam like the ends of the plants our mother pinches off, saying, "Grow, grow, damn you."

Days it rained, we'd hear Miles's snores even after we came home from school, but on clear mornings the sound of him revving his pickup truck to keep it from stalling in the side yard's worn-away grass would wake us. What woke us at night was the loose loud slur of Miles's voice, or the stumble of his feet over the porch steps as he and our mother came home from wherever it was they'd gone.

Our mother and grandmother would splash glasses of tap water over Miles and Jamie when they got at each other, Miles usually getting at Jamie a lot more than Jamie could get at Miles, on account of his arms' length and the strength in even that four-and-a-half-fingered hand. Once they were getting at each other so much, unbalancing a lamp and banging into the coffee table, our grandmother fetched the broom from the broom closet and smacked them both with the flat of it, near cracking its handle over someone's wet shoulder or back, while she and our mother, tugging someone else's furious red fist until it slipped loose, screamed at them to stop.

Mindy and I never did do much more than watch.

"Almost thought I'd forgot what it's like to have a man in the house," our mother, tipping back to her mouth the last trickle of tap water from a glass, said to our grandmother.

Our grandmother righted the lamp and kneed the coffee table into its proper place.

Somewhere in the house—upstairs, the back hall, the cellar—hard to tell—a door slammed.

But Miles one night didn't come home to park his

pickup truck in the side yard, and to none of us but all of us our mother said, again pulling back the curtain to confirm the bare patch his truck had over a few weeks made, "Don't think I didn't know." We were all tucked against the table in our chairs, waiting for our grandmother to bring the supper to it. Many of the times after Jamie and Miles got at each other Jamie would not come home for supper either, and so we wondered if this time Jamie had got at Miles the most before our mother and grandmother poured the water, and if he would, like Jamie, come home late, in a huffing sort of sulk, clipping the back door barely shut behind him to creep up the stairs almost too quietly to catch, though our mother, sitting up in the dark, could always hear these things and would catch him anyway.

My eyes looked at Mindy's and then to Jamie's, though his gave away nothing that he might have known.

"Oh, I knew," our mother said.

There was a pack of cigarettes that Miles had kept in the refrigerator, and there was a lopsided pair of scuffed and heelworn boots that Miles had left kicked into a corner of the hall, but our mother said that no, he would not be back, not even to collect his things.

"Him?" she said, smiling out smoke from her mouth.

She coaxed a deep-voiced laugh from deep in her chest.

We saw the cigarettes in the refrigerator for only a few days before they were gone, and Mindy thought that Miles had come back and taken them no matter what our mother had said. "No," I told her, and that afternoon pointed out to her Jamie, out back at the edge of the woods behind our house, breathing out smoke of his

6

own, while his lips shaped shapes we thought might be new things he was thinking to say to the girl he keeps tied in the woods.

We don't know who the girl our brother keeps tied to a tree in the woods is. We don't know what the girl looks like. We would like to think she is pretty, and Mindy says, in the quiet after-bedtime darkness of our bedroom some nights, that she would prefer the tied-up girl's hair a pale shade of blonde, perhaps tied with a green ribbon, but never a bow.

We know our brother has told his friends. Pressed against the stickered surface of his door when they're all shut inside his bedroom, we've heard them talk. We've heard the words "gorgeous," "wicked," "pound on you," "no way," "not yet." We've heard other words, and words we couldn't make out, and the simple rough grunting and smacking of boys hitting other boys hard with their hands and, possibly, their feet.

We wonder who else knows. We've tried to count the girls in our school, in our brother's older grade—the girls testing each other's eyeshadow in the hallways, the girls whose bra straps the boys reach to snap in class, the girls old enough for a Saturday afternoon permanent or a pair of pierced ears if they want one, and some of them do—but can't tell if any one of these girls is missing. They walk down the halls of school and we watch them, counting them silently to ourselves, noting in a notebook their numbers—there are so many of them, these older girls. We study a blush-bruised face, note a hand's chipped fingernail polish, observe the hand-beaded bracelets knotted around their wrists, memorize the careful line lipstick has left at the corner of a frown, tally the unbuttoned buttons of their blouses, practice their practiced walks.

We don't know who the girl is.

Downstairs, dressed, hair gathered into ponytails, socks tugged on, eyes rubbed and red, we wait for more news. Our grandmother has tipped over the chairs in the living room as if she might find our brother beneath. "Lit the fire and then left," she says. She shakes her head. "Just left, I guess." She looks at the woodstove. She holds the broom in her hand. She has swept a pile into the middle of the floor. "Watch where you step," she says. I watch her watch where we step.

The chairs look the way the chairs looked when we used to make forts, or caves, or sunken ships, Jamie heaving them over for us to crawl beneath.

"Squeeze this!" he'd dare us, holding out his arm, clenching his fist, and showing all his teeth. Under the skin of his arm a hard bump trembled. "Feel that?"

Our mother stands at the kitchen window, cupping a hand to the glass and peering out. Inside, we can barely hear the rain. The fire in the stove snaps. "He's somewhere," our mother says. "Somewhere out there. Probably somewhere inside a house, knowing him."

"Take the flashlight in case you need it," she says.

"There's still some oatmeal on the stove," she says.

"Don't forget a jacket," she says. "A scarf, maybe."

"Well, you'd better get going," she says.

"Aren't you going?" she says.

Our grandmother kneels to sweep up the clots of dust and hair.

❄

Each afternoon, when the tied-up girl watches the sun's red smear through the trees, she shivers. This is what we think. We think she shivers, thinking of the cold night to come. Shivers, thinking of the deep darkness and how quiet it gets in the dark woods at night in the fall, when the only sound is the sound of her blood in her ears, a sound that sounds louder the more she thinks of it.

Has our brother brought her blankets? We've checked closets, toppling the stacks our grandmother folds the towels into, hunting for the ripped and raggedy blankets our mother says at this point are only useful for spreading out in the yard to lie on. And sometimes, lying awake in our own bed, we worry: what of roaming and collarless dogs, forecasts for frost, the long wait for sunrise, the man that Sarah Quinn said she saw carrying a knife in the neighborhood? How does a girl sleep, standing up, against the rough bark of a tree, in the cold quiet dark of the woods at night? How does she go to the bathroom?

Jamie showed us how to stack five or six or seven pennies on our elbows and quick-snap our arms to catch them. He showed us how to give the Indian sunburn, demonstrating first on my arm and then on Mindy's. He showed us how to steal packets of sugar from Mike's on the way home from school and to keep them in our jacket pockets for when we were hungry, or, he said, in case we got lost in the woods. He showed us where the trails in the woods went, and how some connected, and why others looked the same but weren't the same, and whose backyards the trails ended at. He showed us how to fit a chain back onto the bicycle it had fallen off of. He pulled aside the low branches of Mrs. Mathews's bushes to show us the white mothballs tucked in the grass and woodchips there, and said that even if Chris Cervini told us they were ivory, they were not. He showed us the way to fan a paper book of matches and light them all at once—he called it a kind of cocktail. He showed Mindy how to shape a fist so she wouldn't break her thumb when she threw it, and showed me how to turn my shoulder toward a punch.

He did not show us how to steal pouches of Apple Jack from the store or how to tuck it into our cheeks or how to shoot brown spit through our teeth at someone else's new white sneakers. He did not show us how to breathe to light a cigarette, or how to inhale its smoke without coughing. He did not show us which kids sell strings of firecrackers for a dollar. He did not show us how to take three pink pieces of chewed-together gum from our mouths and rub it into Sarah Quinn's hair so that the next day she would have to come to school with a boy's haircut and small red ears. He did not show us how to use a pocketknife to cut off a toad's leg. But these things too we learned in time.

Our feet are the first parts of us to get good and wet. But soon what we wear turns darker, hangs heavy—the trailing cuff of a pantleg, the tops of our shoulders, the drooping ends of our sleeves.

"It'll take more than that to melt you," our mother said, twisting the umbrella from my hand just before we left. She opened the door for us. The spring stretched tight. By the time we circled around back to try the back door, ducking below the windows our mother could spy us out from, the knob was already locked.

We sidestep the root-ruined sidewalk squares and head down the street. We do not see any people. What we see is the mostly yellow grass footing wire fences, two dented tipped-over cans spilling newspaper and chicken bones, yellow and brown leaves banked and blown and now shiny with water, orange and red leaves that cork-screw quickly down through the rain. The leaves smell of rot. The leaves stick to our shoes. The leaves clog the sewer drains and float on the water flooding the curbs.

Our mother has never sent us to hunt up Jamie, and we don't know where to begin to look. We hop puddles to the houses where dogs don't bark, to knock on doors and ask for him. "He's probably somewhere inside a house," Mindy says.

I make Mindy walk in front of me. When she turns around to see if I'm still following her, I say, "Walk."

"Go to that house and ask if he is inside," I tell her. It is a white house with a white fence and a driveway nicely swept of leaves. I watch Mindy unlatch the gate, watch her walk up to the door. Blinking, I inspect the clouds for signs of a possible break in the weather.

"He is not inside," Mindy says, coming back.

There are, along these streets, within even these few hilly blocks of potholes and trees we call our neighbor-hood, so many houses—here a half-hung shutter, here a chimney's relaxed pitch, here a porch light still palely burning, here a push mower left to rust in the rain—all the curtained windows, all the closed doors. There are so many houses it is hard to figure for sure where our brother might be, or might have been. There are so many houses we wonder how many doors we will have to an-nounce ourselves at to ask after our brother.

We think of the places, if not inside a house, Jamie could be: the scoop of muddy dirt beneath the back porch, the crook of the tree behind Joe Letourneau's garage, walking in a stream to keep a dog from tracking his scent, behind the school bouncing a ball off the bricks.

"He is not inside," Mindy says.

"He is in the woods," Mindy says.

Our mother did not send us to find Miles when he did not come home for supper. She did not wake us too early the next morning to search for him in the neighborhood. After another day or two of—when she thought we wouldn't notice—looking to see if there was, perhaps, a pickup truck parked in the side yard's worn-away grass, she said, "Ought to get some grass seed for that dirt patch." But she did not send us to the hardware store with a dollar or two for a sack of seed.

What our grandmother said about Miles, some night not long after he didn't come home, was, "He's not the kind to tie the knot."

She had said this same thing about many of the men our mother found and brought home, and even, once or twice, about our mother.

"No, but he's the kind to tie one on," our mother said, laughing another bubbly cough from her chest. She mashed her cigarette out in the ashy saucer next to her plate and uncrossed her legs. Jamie forked up another mouthful of our grandmother's potatoes and gravy. He swallowed. He scrubbed his mouth with his napkin and fisted it into a paper lump. He pushed his plate away.

"Can I please be excused?" he asked.

"*May* I," our grandmother said, her cigarette bobbing

between her lips as she thumbed her lighter three times for a flame. "*May* I please be excused."

When we first found out that our brother keeps a girl tied to a tree in the woods, we did not think to tell anyone. We imagined he would tell them all, at supper, when our mother asked us what we might have learned or done or not done that day, in the way of lessons or trouble or chores. But when Miles was there it was him our mother asked of, and once Miles had left Jamie had little cause to say anything at supper beyond "Please pass the salt."

We thought to see her for ourselves. One afternoon after school we spied Jamie out from the upstairs window as he picked up a whittled stick and walked into the woods. We ran down through the house and out through the snarls of weedy growth behind our house to the edge of the woods. We watched Jamie from behind a tree. We saw the back of his t-shirt vanish down a trail, the tip of his stick slashing at low-hung leaves.

At the first fork we headed right. Mindy placed an ear to the ground, and came up with dirt in her hair. She touched a finger to her lips and pointed. We soft-stepped over old leaves, twigs, curls of birch paper. We stayed low. We did not jostle a branch. We kept our heads. We counted the side trails on our fingers. We watched. We listened. We waited.

We waited longer.

I gave Mindy ten fingers for a view.

"He's gone," Mindy whispered.

Jamie, pulling from his pocket two pieces of rope, showed us how to tie a stevedore's knot, a sheepshank, a hangman's noose, a cat's paw, a lariat loop, a clove hitch, a double sheet bend.

"Jamie's the kind to tie the knot," Mindy said.

But Jamie said that a girl never has a head for two things—directions and rope.

"No girl I've ever known," he said.

"No, not even either of you," he said.

"Of course, all you really need to know is your basic square knot," he said.

He said that we'd forget every knot he ever looped and undid and looped again, pulling the ropes tight, cinching the ends, to show us how. He said that we would never remember the trails he showed us in the woods, or how they connected, or why some looked the same as others, or whose backyards the trails ended at.

"Of course, the best things aren't on the trails," he said.

"I'll show you again, if you want," he said.

"No, like this," he said.

"See?" he said.

"Forget it," he said. "Just stick with me."

We often wonder who else—besides us and Jamie's friends—knows about the girl our brother keeps tied to a tree in the woods. We believe, sometimes, that we have heard rumors among the kids who ride the school bus out to the end of Old Reservoir Road. Mindy tries to hear the whispers two boys share at the corner of the schoolyard's painted-on kickball diamond. I look for penciled words on desktops or folded notes dropped in the hallway.

We believe there are boys who meet in someone's cobwebby cellar. The boys draw their plans in the sawdust on the cracked cement floor. The boys pass each other messages written in code and sketch maps in invisible ink that shows only against a candle flame, or if you dip the paper in lemon water, or if you breathe on it for ten minutes. The boys head into the woods with binoculars and penknives, with compasses and walkie-talkies, with canteens and waterproof matches, with rope of their own. They rattle the dried goldenrod stalks with sticks, imitate the hooting of owls, hunt among the trees for the girl they have heard is tied to one.

Sometimes we worry that they will find her some windy afternoon when our brother is shut in his bedroom, doing whatever it is that he does in there.

From sidewalk to woods is a distance not more than a person's front yard, house, and backyard, if we find the right backyard where one of the trails begins, but in the woods where the rain-raked trees have lost their leaves we know we'll only get wetter than we already are.

We keep walking through the neighborhood.

A brief spell of hard rain falls. We wait it out on the porch of a house where no one answers the doorbell that Mindy, because she cannot hear it chime, presses twice. We wonder if, somewhere in the woods, Jamie is holding the umbrella over the head of the girl he keeps tied to a tree.

"Jamie," Mindy calls out. "Jamie!"

There is a chance, we agree, that Jamie will be behind the school in the rain, thinking of how to rescue his ball from the gymnasium's flat roof, where he has accidentally thrown it. There is a chance he is at the store to buy some candy for the girl he keeps tied up, or to buy her a magazine he can hold up and flip for her to see the photos of, or to buy her a carton of chocolate milk to share while they wait for the rain to end.

There is a chance, even, that Jamie is by now back at home, his wet things placed on the hearth beside the fire he built hours ago—a good chance, we agree, that he is in his bed, dreaming of his tied-up girl and all the secret things he will tell her.

"May I hold your hand?" could be one of them.

Rain drips from the ends of Mindy's soaked ponytails, and, I guess, from mine.

Our sneakers seep water when we step.

"Home?" Mindy asks.

"Home," I say.

What I want to know, waking sometimes to an early light and lying back against my sleep-squashed pillow with my arms behind my head while beside me under the blankets Mindy breathes, is does the girl our brother keeps tied up in the woods struggle to get loose from the knots binding her to the tree? Does she rub the rope against the tree she's tied to? Does she work her cold fingers to a place where they can pick an end of rope free? Do the forest animals hear her crying and, coming to see why she is sad, chew through the knots our brother has practiced so often that he says he can tie them one-handed in the dark?

Or does the girl not mind being tied to the tree? Does our brother bring her the things she wants, and does she like the quiet of the woods, the long low slant of sifted sun and then the hours of mottled moonlight, better than the four walls of her bedroom, the days of desks and chalk dust?

❄

Back at home, what we do not expect is for the front door to be locked, for our mother's car to be gone from the driveway, for the chimney to show no smoke, for our own house to be as quiet and empty as most every other house we have walked to this morning to test a doorbell or rap a knuckle.

We check the knob of the back door—still locked— then see if any of the windows might be open.

"Who leaves a window open in the rain?" is what I think to say to Mindy, but, rain dripping down me, lift her on ten fingers to try anyway.

We ring the doorbell. We knock.

"Grocery shopping?" I say. "Laundromat?"

"Getting their hair done?" Mindy says.

"Too early," I say.

We try the doorbell again, pushing it so long my fingertip turns white.

And then there is nothing to do or say except what Mindy says: "We still haven't checked the woods."

Does the girl, awake some night in the woods, feel a terrible thirst, and wish herself home to stumble half-asleep from bed to bathroom's yellow light, where she runs the faucet for a minute before gulping up cold water in her two cupped hands?

Does she plot, during those long hours of darkness, how to trick our brother so that she can escape and somehow tie him to the tree, using the same knots she has watched him shape?

Does our brother bring her fresh clothes to wear?

Does he turn his back while she changes, or does he watch? Would she run if, while she changed her clothes, he kept his back turned, like a gentleman would?

We think, sometimes, Mindy and I, that we would know the answers to all of our questions about the girl our brother keeps tied to a tree if only we could know her name.

Tree trunks black with rain, bush-snagged leaves, every branch's hem of drops, a path's single slippery rain-slicked rock: into the woods we go.

"I don't know" was what Jamie told me when I once asked him who had first made these trails, who had figured out the shortest way to circle a hill out of sight from a house's top-floor window, who had cut back the pricker bushes, who had beaten down the weeds.

"Indians?" Mindy had asked.

The trail, buried under wet and bunched leaves, is hard to follow. With a sogged sneaker toe I scrape away leaves and sticks, candy wrappers and bottlecaps. Bits of glass stud the muddy dirt beneath. Low branches clutch the cellophane sleeves of cigarette packs, and under the orange ferns are the weather-whitened and rain-stuck pages of magazines. A rusted can of spray paint has caught in a tangle of branches. Holding back a branch so it doesn't whip Mindy's face, I take a step forward.

"If we knew her name, we would know the name to call as we walk through these woods," I think to say to Mindy, who instead holds her hands to her mouth and calls, "Jamie!"

❄

We believe a man jogging through the woods one afternoon ran past the girl our brother keeps tied to a tree,
but never saw her. Did he stop to tie a loose shoelace and
look the wrong way, or was he watching only the ground,
to keep from stumbling on a rock? We don't know if she
called out to him, or bit her tongue, or if the noise of his
feet on the pine-needled dirt and the rush of wind in
his ears kept him from thinking that he heard anything
more than one bird calling to another.

In the woods, we can't hear the sound of cars splashing
through puddled streets, can't hear the sound of someone
calling inside a wet dog, can't hear anything except the
stutter of rain against the leaf-covered ground and the
scuff of our own cold feet through soaked leaves.

The light, since we left, has not changed, and it might
be any time at all.

We walk, and keep walking, and still keep walking,
but all we see are leafpiles and bushes and trees with no
girls tied to them.

Mindy has stopped to rummage deep down in her
pockets, where, I see in a moment, the sugar packets she
long ago stuffed are about the only thing about us that
is still dry. And they are slightly damp.

Mindy bends her body over to keep the rain off, rips
a corner, and lifts an envelope up to her mouth. She
empties it in one go. She tears open another.

"It is," our brother once said, "instant energy."

"Can I have one?" I say.

"May I have one?" I say.

�֍

On cold clear nights when wind worries the sashes in our bedroom window, Mindy and I tell ourselves that the girl our brother keeps tied up in the woods has a father out searching for her, a tall father with strong hands and dark eyes. The tied-up girl's father weeps when he sees her old kindergarten photo on the mantel—her white turtleneck with its pattern of tiny hearts, the missing teeth in her smile, her pale blonde hair—and pulls on his boots and walks out into the night, vowing to find his daughter by daybreak, this daughter he has wished to come home for so long.

Other times, when the wind is not so loud, the night not so cold, we tell each other that she has an older brother, a brother who knows the woods as well as Jamie does, a brother who will untie the knots and rub the blood back into her stiff wrists and, holding her hand, lead her back out of the woods.

I blink rain from my eyelashes. I curl my fists as far into my wet pockets as they will go. Next to me, Mindy chatters her teeth and hugs herself. All around us, the black spikes of bare trees lift their limbs into the rain. We have found some bits of what might once have been rope, and a bright yellow rope untied from someone's swingset, and a length of old jumprope missing its handles, but not a girl tied to a tree, and not Jamie.

"He probably took her someplace dry," I say, "someplace to get her out of all this rain."

"Probably did," Mindy shivers out.

"They're probably all home by now," I say.

"Probably are," Mindy says.

"Home?" I say.

"Home," Mindy says.

We walk back through the trees, the broken branches, the fallen limbs, the red-leafed twigs that rain has knocked loose. We follow what looks to be a trail's rocky route, circling ahead through the mostly bare trees. We step through dead ferns and old thorny growth, step over a banged-up street sign post with a clump of concrete still stuck to its end. We hunch our shoulders. We sniffle.

We do not remember seeing the circle of sooty stones, the burst blackened pods of last summer's milkweed, the burned branches scattered about, the crumpled cans, so much broken glass. And we know we have not seen the two boys squatting on their heels, their wet jean jackets pasted to the curves of their backs, their wet hair hanging to hide their faces.

"Have you seen our brother?" I say, thinking one of them might be one of the boys that Jamie at times lets into his room. But when they each look up from the magazine they have been looking at, I can tell that they are older than Jamie and his friends, old enough to have wisps of hair at the corners of their mouths, old enough to smoke on the street where anyone might see them, old enough to go to the older school and so not have heard about the girl our brother keeps tied to a tree. One boy's jeans are ripped at the knee, and I can see part of his leg. He folds the wet magazine shut, rolls it up, and tucks it under his ripped jacket. His brown eyes, looking at us, squint against the rain, and tiny beads of water have caught in his dark lashes.

"Maybe," he says, standing up.

"Who's your brother?" the other boy asks us.

"What are you two doing out here?" the first boy wants to know.

The girl our brother keeps tied to a tree has spent clear nights counting the stars. She knows that in another week, once the weather breaks, she'll she'll recognize every star anyone might see from the middle of the dark woods. She has spent afternoons watching birds flick through low branches, scatter leaves with their beaks, and, at sunset, flock to roost in the branches above her. When the wind is still and the dried leaves no longer rattle, she can sometimes hear a back door latching shut somewhere in our neighborhood beyond the woods, or a pulley squeaking under an old sash cord as someone forces a window up, or someone's mother's voice added to the air to summon someone for supper.

She has looked forward to the sun rising red through a morning haze more times than she cares to think.

"He keeps her tied to a tree," I hear myself say.

"No, only that she's somewhere in the woods," I believe I also say.

"Don't you think we'd untie her, then?" I seem to ask.

"If we knew, we'd go there, since that's where our brother'd be," I may say.

"Well, I guess we'll try," I think I say next.

"No, we already looked over that way," I say, or consider saying.

But what I wish I have said is nothing.

❄

Somewhere in the woods, the girl our brother keeps tied to a tree waits. She has waited all night, all morning, the rain soaking her pale blonde hair. Her hands and feet are nearly numb, and she hopes that soon Jamie will come to untie her, will hold her hand and wrap a dry coat around her shoulders while he shows her the trail that leads from the woods, the trail so covered by the rain-ragged leaves that no one else can see it. She wishes that he will build a fire for her the way he lit one for us this morning. But Jamie does not come, Jamie does not untie her, Jamie does not guide her from the woods, Jamie does not build a fire.

And so we lead the older boys away from her. Because we can't find her, we know that wherever we walk through the woods will not be the place where she is tied.

"A little more this way," Mindy tells the two boys.

"I think over here," I say.

Soon she can no longer hear the sound of our feet and the older boys' feet tramping through all the fallen leaves. The woods are quiet, and she can hear only an airplane far above her, or a bird calling from a branch, or the steady patter of rain. She cannot hear us walking into the woods, cannot hear the older boys following us, cannot hear their heavy steps as they stumble on roots and branches, cannot hear their heavy breath just over our shoulders.

The rain has slowed. The clouds seem darker, and the trees. There is a wind. The wind smells of smoke, of all the smoke rising from the chimneys of the houses in our neighborhood beyond the woods. The boys have brushed their wet hair from their dark faces. They have taken off their belts. The tree presses against my back. A few feet away, Mindy stands against another tree, her hands also snared by her sides, and I pretend that I cannot hear the things she is saying, the sounds she is making.

"Like this?" the boy at my tree asks, working the yellow swingset rope in his hands.

"I guess," I can barely whisper.

"Can I?" the other boy says, coming over from Mindy's tree to mine.

In the darkening woods, after we have passed, the tied-up girl hears boys: boys shaking the raindrops from the bushes for a sign of her, boys carrying hand-sketched maps and sharpened sticks, boys hooting among the trees like owls, even older boys with magazines they have stolen from their fathers and carried into the woods to study. Then she is glad of the ropes, glad that Jamie's careful knots hold her so tightly against the tree's pebbled bark, glad that she can hide against the tree in the middle of the woods, this tree that has for weeks shed its leaves upon her. She holds her breath. She does not move her feet. She waits. She knows that the boys will tire in the damp dusk's spitting rain, will grow bored of searching for her in wet woods, will punch each other's arms as they follow the muddy trails toward the windowed lights of home. She knows that only after supper, when the rains have ended and the clouds have cleared, will they again think of her, that only as they lie in their beds listening to the restless, nervous winds will they imagine how tomorrow they will return to the woods, hunting for the tree she is tied to.

# THE BURNING HOUSE

A town of crooked sidewalks, hills, a strip of orange
behind trees where each night I watched the sun
go down—this happened—all of this—in the town I
thought was named for my mother, or else the town, I
thought later, for which my mother had been named.

Still later, neither of these turned out to be true.

A tumble of barn along the roadside, goldenrod in a
field, the smell of smoke from what we burned, season to
season, stirring ash with sooty sticks: these things were
our town.

On maps taken from the glovebox of my mother's car,
maps spread and crinkled across our kitchen's bare floor,
soft and torn on folds, faded with age, I studied other

25

towns and the large letters of cities. I traced the lines of roads with my finger, reading the names of places.

"Heartwellville," I might have said, or, "Claverack."

"Claverack?" my mother would say, walking by, each step a hundred miles. "Do you think you'd like it there?"

In our house, in our town, everything creaked—feet on wooden floors, bottoms on wooden chairs, wood doors on rusty hinges, the wood frame of our house as it settled.

In a wind, the trees outside my window.

Anytime, the joints and bones of our town's old, stepping and shuffling in and out of the post office, led by leashed dogs along our roads, rustling to kneel in the pews at church.

In our town, to me, everyone was old.

Afternoons, I walked from the end of the bus route to Phyllis's house, to the house where Phyllis lived with the mother few people in our town remembered. In Phyllis's house even almost daily, I too did not know, though I was too young, then, to have forgotten. I followed the tipped squares of sidewalk away from the school-bus turnaround until they changed into dirt paths, rotting fenceposts, dry weeds, a plowed-under field.

The carpet in Phyllis's house was thick with Sweety's hair. White clumps of it clung to curtains and armchair, rolled in ropes across the kitchen linoleum. In the light of Phyllis's TV, I watched the twist and curl of her cigarette's blue smoke with Sweety's hairs, what looked to me like a kind of dance. Cookies Phyllis baked tasted of Sweety's hair, and afternoons spent at Phyllis's house I spent hungry, which was every afternoon—afternoons of dragging feet and ticking clocks, glasses of tap water and breath-fogged windows.

Sweety, when he saw me, stayed away, and then afternoons were a hunt under the couch, in the broom closet, behind ticking radiators. Or, when Phyllis tired of knocking feet and sighing lips, afternoons were branches broken into bits, a spread of dry grass, a handful of gravel hurled and thunked against the garage wall.

Afternoons, always, were waiting for the sound of tires in Phyllis's driveway, for the glow of headlights through Phyllis's windows, for the sound of my mother's voice at Phyllis's door.

This was fall, and winter, and spring, and always what the smell was was burning things.

I am no longer sure of memory, of the flashes I see and also of the gaps where I know things are missing; if what I recall is recalled for any reason beyond the telling. What is told becomes what is until it is told again. Even then, years back, what I knew was less a story than an occasion for telling.

The story in the post office of our town—a counter where Sylvia dropped nickels and dimes into your cupped palm for change, a faded FBI poster, a few rows of boxes Sylvia bundled mail into—among the drivers of RR 1, or, perhaps, RR 2—this story, we all found out later, after what happened happened, was that there was an old woman in one of the houses along one of these routes. There were many old women tucked into houses back in the hills, along the roads that in spring turned to soft, rutted mud. This we knew. But this old woman, the drivers—young men with bright yellow US MAIL stickers stuck to their trucks—said, knocked on an upstairs window of the house where, as they did at any other house, they opened the box, lowered the flag, and drove to the next house on the route. Her arm, they said, waved and waved as they drove away, and these drivers said they always waved back to this old woman who waited, every day, for them to come.

Wednesday night bingo games at the church hall, that one winter—so I was told, sometime else—some of our town's old said, "Wish it was me who'd started it. Would've if I'd known."

Phyllis's house was, she claimed, a house of one rule only. "The refrigerator," Phyllis had told me, one afternoon early on, swinging its door wide on a glass bottle of milk, shapes wrapped in tinfoil and cellophane, sticks of butter stacked like bricks, "is right here if you get hungry. The glasses and plates are up there, the forks and spoons are in here. Whatever you want, just make like you're at home. Okay?"

I nodded.

"The only thing I ask," Phyllis said, "is that you don't go upstairs."

Later, when my mother had come to claim me and we stood by the door, I saw the carpeted stairs, covered in Sweety's hair, leading up to an upstairs hall where, I thought, a strip of wallpaper hung peeled from the wall. A shade seemed to be drawn over a window, and in the dark I saw what looked like stacks of books, or rows of boxes, at the top of the stairs.

For a house in our town, Phyllis's house was—before it was not—a big house.

✳

Nights were me, the wide seat of my mother's Ford, and my mother, holding the wheel in her hands. That wheel turned and turned as we drove the back roads home from Phyllis's house. Our legs vanished into the dark at our feet, our faces lit up green from the dashboard. This time was what I dreamed of in school. I dreamed this pulling my brown paper bag from my desk and lining up to walk to the lunchroom, I dreamed this sitting on the hill above the kickball diamond, I dreamed this under rows of fluorescent lights while Miss Jackson told us about the way the gravity from the sun pulled the earth in tight circles around it. In winter, Miss Jackson said, this pull made the days shorter, the nights longer.

Gravity pulled my mother's Ford down the hill to our house, dark and quiet in the valley. We stepped inside to dark rooms. My mother crumpled newspaper into balls, packing them into the woodstove, while I flicked on lamps, my feet creaking across floors that had not been walked on all day. From the other room I heard the squeak of the damper being turned, the rush of air sucked into the woodstove.

"Do you need a sweater?" my mother might have said, or, "Peas or carrots tonight?"

Nights were a hunt across maps for the town that would someday take me. Nights were my mother's face by lamplight, the turn of a page, a strand of my mother's hair tucked behind an ear, the sound of words spoken in my mother's voice.

The night of the fire, I stood to the side while for a time my mother stood near to Phyllis, where many others stood, also. Snowed in, no one had left home for days, but most of our town soon gathered, even our town's old, who toiled through deep drifts. Wes Gaines, our town's policeman, stood near to me, in packed snow, his arms crossed, the metal he wore glowing in the light. His cruiser was parked closest to what was Phyllis's house of all the cars parked along the road, and its lights still spun red and blue across trees, snow, all of our faces. The red and blue lights vanished when they spun past what we all fronted.

"Could be anything," Wes Gaines said to some man of our town he stood near to as well. "Creosote, bad wiring, insurance fraud, arson." He sniffed and spat into the snow. "Who knows?"

The heat blazed on our faces. Inside bulky winter coats, we sweated. We squinted our eyes, and some of our town, closer than I was, held out gloveless hands, rubbing and turning them over and over.

I watched Wes Gaines. Wes Gaines watched the flames. Wes Gaines watched Phyllis. Wes Gaines watched the pack of boys who stood alone, pointing and laughing, shoulders hunched. His eyes were moving all the time. When Phyllis left what was left of her house she left in the back of Wes Gaines's cruiser, the way Phyllis's mother had left, earlier, in the back of the county ambulance.

By the time Phyllis left, those of us still watching were few. By dawn, they said, when the snow turned blue in the light, only one or two people of our town, and one of the volunteer firefighters who'd come too late, still watched the smoking embers and blackened frame.

❆

Phyllis did not hear me—or, if she did hear me, gave no sign of it—as I crept down the creaking stairs from the attic to the second floor, or down the carpeted stairs from the second floor to the first. My hands, held out, touched rough wallpaper, patches of bare plaster. In my own ears all I heard was the rush and pulse of my own quickened blood. The echo of the voice was already gone. Snow hushed every sound.

Phyllis, when I walked into the kitchen where our last hands lay face down on the table near puddles of melted wax, was standing by the window, her hands cupped to the glass. Outside, the sky sifted down in white.

"Your mother's going to have some time getting through this," she said, turning to me. "Must be six inches already."

My mother paid Phyllis every other Friday, a sealed envelope I carried to school, tucked between sock and shoe. When I walked to Phyllis's house on every other Fridays, I gave her this envelope. Phyllis's cigarette would tip up in her lips, glowing bright, as she ripped open the envelope with a fingernail and shuffled through the bills inside. A flash of green was all I ever saw.

Sometimes, on every other Fridays, what Phyllis had for me was a plate of fly-flicked brownies, or a bowl of popcorn soggy with melted butter, dusted with Sweety's hair. In the quiet of Phyllis's kitchen, my chair tucked into table, my paper napkin balled in my fist, whatever Phyllis had made untouched in front of me, I heard sounds not the sounds of TV but of something else: a tap, a thump—the sounds, or what I thought were the sounds, of someone testing walls, rattling a doorknob, knocking floors for trapdoors.

❄

If, in telling this story, who I am does not at times sound like me, it may not be me speaking. Everyone in our town has seen most of, or part of, what I have seen; everyone in our town has argued these spectacles over the counter at Agway or in the booths at Rose's coffee shop, and their voices creep and blur into my own. In our town, sooner or later—sooner, most often—everyone sounds like everyone else. A word means anything, everything, nothing. What we say is "Yes," "No," "Possibly," letting these sounds carry the weight we dare not.

All these things I have imagined for years, turning events over and over in my mind until what happened was lost somewhere I could no longer reach.

"The clues," said the woman reporter we watched, long ago, on TV, "are few, and local authorities say they don't add up."

I ask myself: some old turpentine-soaked rags in the basement, a lightning strike, a splash of gasoline and a match, a fireplace log rolling across a brick hearth, the hushed breath of spontaneous combustion?

What happened happened during a time of snow, a time when the smell of what we burned—wood, oil—caught in our hair and in our clothes. What happened happened all at once, so that later, the old of our town, sitting spring nights on porches, could argue about what happened, exactly, or did not happen, or was believed to have happened.

"Early frosts, ice storms, and dry summers," the people of our town said, peering outside at the falling snow, "and now this." In the blizzard we stayed shut indoors for days, weeks it could have been, the roads blocked by drifts where stuck cars slept, or else, the people said, where bodies frozen stiff and blue waited for the cold to break.

"Who," they asked each other on party line calls, "who has seen Tom Thompson?"

Or was it in dry summer, the time of cicadas and grass scorched yellow, of wells gone dry and the reservoirs low, a time when everything was ready to burn?

What we knew were extremes, and these, more than what happened, stay with me.

Our town was a town of closed doors, a town of curtained windows.

In Phyllis's house, one door opened into a room piled with boxes, old magazines, skis, junked stereo speakers. Curtains pulled back to a sweep of gravel road, a view of spruce trees, the slope to the swamp.

Phyllis watched TV through its flip and roll, smoking each cigarette to the filter, getting up to adjust the antennae. I sat on the floor, knees hunched to chin, studying the grain of wood in the floorboards, the plants along Phyllis's windowsill, the snowed TV screen.

Phyllis, to me, was old, though not as old as Phyllis's mother, who lived upstairs in Phyllis's house. Phyllis's mother I saw only from outside—a hand parting a curtain when I thought she thought I couldn't see, the reflection of light off a pair of eyeglasses.

I imagined what anyone would have imagined. Cobwebs like lace, the scent of dust, a white sweater, soft folds of skin. I had heard Phyllis say she was crazy.

✺

Many things my mother told me. "Phyllis's perm makes her look older," she said once, driving the back roads home from Phyllis's house.

"What a long day," she said to me, most days, as if our days still stretched behind us, fading into distance.

"Saw Miss Jackson at the I.G.A. this afternoon, and she says you're doing well in school," she told me another time, and I marveled at the thought of Miss Jackson in the I.G.A., pushing a cart of food on spinning wheels.

Later, one time we were driving from our house to somewhere else and passed the place where Phyllis's house had been, my mother looked, out of the corners of her eyes, at what was left of Phyllis's house, which by then wasn't much.

This was how my mother had come to look at me, afterward. From where I sat with my maps, or shading a drawing, I would feel her behind me—glancing sideways, I imagined, at the strokes of my pencil, or the holes in my socks. Those days, she seemed always to verge on telling me something. I would look up at her—framed by a doorway, or turning back to her newspaper—and watch her mouth, which shaped a strange smile as she shook her head. Whatever it was, she never spoke it.

But in the car, that afternoon, I too looked at what was left of Phyllis's house. I looked at the side of my mother's face, the tiny wrinkles in the corner of her eye, from, I thought, so much straining to see. After a moment, my mother said to me, "Why did you never tell me?"

The afternoon of the blizzard was an afternoon of five-card draw, of Phyllis's greasy deck and a bowl of salted peanuts, of candles glowing on the kitchen table because,

34

Phyllis said, the power lines were down, weighted with all that snow. We bet pennies from Phyllis's tobacco jar, raising and calling and laying our hands down.

"Showdown," Phyllis said, tossing her penny on the pile between us, tapping ash from her cigarette.

"Royal Flush," I said, "I think."

Outside, wet snow swirled past Phyllis's windows, collecting in the crooks of branches. Her curtains she had pulled open so we could see the plows, lights spinning in early dark. A clink of chains was all we heard as they passed, though this sound, anyone in our town could have said, was like the other sounds we all heard nights we lay awake in bed—the tap of a branch against the roof, rain ticking on the window, the hiss of a radiator—any sound reminding us of all those things we'd forgotten.

Did I mention the name of my mother, the name of this place, the name anyone can see on any folded-out map, tracing the red line of the road through our town?

What I leave out every time, what I never know how to say, or even approach saying, is Phyllis's attic—which is to say, really, Phyllis's mother. Would anyone believe me if I told how Phyllis kept the door at the top of the attic stairs padlocked? No one, I tell myself, would trust this story I tell, this story I have tried to tell so many times, of a young boy, of a town and a house and an old woman and a snowstorm and a fire; no one would believe existed what I said I had seen. Would it be enough for me to admit that I knew not why any of this was but only that it was? And can anyone believe that on an afternoon of wet snow stuck to everything in and over this town, that on such an afternoon in the hush of no electricity, of snow so thick it muffled the least sound, that I crept up those narrow stairs, unheard, and heard, on the other side of that door, on the other side of that scratched and gouged wood, a voice?

Wouldn't anyone want to know what the voice said to me, or what I heard it say?

Most important, I ask: Would I, now, coming to this story for the first time, believe any of these things myself?

Many people have been to our town. At first the parade of cars was filled with people from the towns around our own, or from the two states our town is cornered between. Later, I sat on the sidewalk, studying license plates, figuring miles on my fingers. On a slip of paper pulled from my pocket I copied down the states: Pennsylvania, I wrote, its blue familiar, and Vermont, and Maryland once, and another time Rhode Island, the smallest state in the nation—all the people, my mother said, who'd caught the broadcast on TV the week before.

"Who," she asked me, "would have ever thought we'd make national news?"

Our town is a town with a story—this we heard on that same broadcast—but I would tell you that the story of our town is not the story of Phyllis's mother, or the story of Phyllis's house. The story of our town is not the story of what happened, or of what happened later, but of what can happen. The story is, really, our town itself, which is to say that the story is about any town.

News came fast over the party lines, or to the houses downtown with their own lines, and later I wondered if some of the light in the sky was shining from our town's telephone wires, stretched and burning too with the hurried breaths of voices.

"Come on," my mother said, setting down the phone. "Get your boots on, and a scarf."

For days I had stared through frost-patterned glass, watching clear blue skies. With my mother these no-school days, I had snipped glossy pictures from magazines and glued them to construction paper, or sifted dry beans in my hands while she simmered soups, the house filling with steam and the smell of onions. On the kitchen table we had spread a deck of concentration cards, lifting a red ladybug where we expected a yellow tulip, or a tiger peering through green grass. Now, tugging at my boots, I watched my mother run through snow—shoveled and unshoveled, drifted and smoothed by the winds that for days had blown over our town, lifting snow back into the sky where the sun shining through it was the light of the prism on Miss Jackson's classroom window. My mother brushed off the roof of the Ford, cleared windows, and climbed inside to warm the engine. In a minute she was back, her face red, her hair smelling of cold.

"Hurry," she said.

Later—two summers, or three, when to recall Phyllis's face was like a dream—what I remember was the green. All along the charred timbers, all across that circle of ashy earth, blackberry bushes had sent runners, new and green as they twined around a brick or a length of wood. Vines and leaves climbed the old frame of the house. Weeds spilled from the tumbled chimney. Goldenrod and ragweed pressed around the foundation, asters waved in the wind. Where I thought I remembered a kitchen, a game of cards, rows of maple seedlings pushed through rotted shingles still black from smoke and heat.

Or is the real story of our town, I sometimes ask myself, the story of how a person can so easily, so quickly, be forgotten in the press of papers and faces and voices in which we all, all of us, daily drown ourselves?

I never knew if Phyllis ran, piling Sweety and some socks and underwear into her car and speeding down the newly cleared roads, escaping to some other town like our town, where a woman like Phyllis would not be much cause for comment; or if there was a trial the judge had thrown out, he said, for want of evidence; or if somehow she had just plain moved away, renting a U-Haul like anyone else would have, though she'd had precious little to load into it.

Phyllis may have even stayed on a year or two in one of the rooms for rent downtown, sitting by her window over Main Street while rain fell, or leaves cluttered the air, or dirty snow, even, lay in banks and piles along the sidewalk—watching our town's old shuffle past, heads bowed all the same. She may have become one of the women out on RR 1 or RR 2, lifting faded clothes to a line, picking crabapples in a paper bag, raising hens in her front yard.

My mother, after the fire, never spoke to me of Phyllis. My mother never voiced Phyllis's name. Not even did my mother say, "That woman," as I had heard certain others in our town do.

I never asked.

My mother said, "I guess you're old enough now to stay home after school by yourself."

I took the slip of paper from my pocket, the pencil marks faded to almost nothing, and in the dark of my room mouthed the words I knew by heart then, and still know now: Pennsylvania, Vermont, Maryland, Rhode Island.

Phyllis's house, burning, lit the sky over our town.

By the time Phyllis had run the half mile to Dotty McRae's, by the time the pump truck came from the next town, volunteer firefighters hanging off the sides, by the time everyone had gathered on the slope above the swamp to watch Phyllis's house burn, by the time the county ambulance had come and gone, its tires spinning on patches of ice, no one thought of what might be saved, or, by the time window glass shattered and the roof collapsed in a shower of sparks, of what might have been saved.

You might think that even days after a blizzard, surrounded by all that water, a house would not burn. But the story whispered among our town's old was that Phyllis's house went up like dry weeds, like seasoned cordwood, like a canful of gasoline.

No one disputed it. We all were there. What we all saw was that heat anyone in our town has wished for on any of our winter nights.

We all, stamping our feet to pack the snow, watched the steam rise and hiss from where a kindled timber fell. Cinders lifted and floated in the air. Phyllis, somewhere in that crowd of us, didn't watch, but sobbed into the hands she held over her face. This was the last time, I believe, that I saw her, though I no longer trust what is merely seen.

The smell of smoke was with us for weeks—has never, really, left us. It is on my fingers, in my hair and my clothes, to this day.

# HISTORY OF
# COLD SEASONS

Where we live: brown weeds lifting from unbroken snow, blown snow rising like smoke. Smoke rising like smoke, thick and white these subzero days, from chimneys. Snow, days old and packed, squeaks underfoot.

My Mattie's feet froze in his boots, the leather laces stiff with ice. When they carried him in, I put his feet against the woodstove, watched while ice hissed and steamed, while water pooled on the hearth, knowing not to bother, knowing already that feeling stopped inches short of what are called "extremities."

Which is not how Mattie would say it.

Dalton, feet under drifted snow and frozen earth, would have said, "Where everything else begins."

Where we live: words take form as I speak them, hanging in the air for anyone to see—my breath visible the instant I exhale it.

I don't speak much, generally.

The searchers—men from town, all of them known to me except those Carl Normandeau called up from Deerfield, leading dogs churning through snow shoulder high, sniffing my Mattie's glove, not barking, as if they knew.

In my kitchen, I scraped frost from the window with a fingernail, watched all the men disappear in blue dusk, spreading apart in a line before they reached the woods. My tea steeped, swirls of color clouding the water. I held the mug in circled hands, warming.

Later, I held those toes in my hands, not warming, the skin blue and under the nails purple. I held them to remember in my hands their shape, to keep with me a feeling he couldn't feel.

Through February and March I chipped at ice dams along the edges of the roof, watched snow warmed by sun slide off—heavy, soft. Icicles dripped deep holes in packed snow. Mattie sat in his chair by the window, quiet, his eyes flicking from one thing to the next.

His cuticles he chewed raw, bloody.

The old sugar house, below the orchard, was where they found him, huddled inside the door, blanketed by snow blown through the chinks, through the windows hunters shot out.

Two, three hours, one of those Deerfield boys told me.

He said other things into his radio while we waited for the ambulance.

Footprints through snow are not difficult to follow. Carl Normandeau wanted the dogs for the newspaper people, whose trucks skidded along my plowed driveway half an hour past dark.

"Mother," my Mattie would say, if he could. What he says when he means "mother" is not a sound anyone else would recognize.

Carl Normandeau, that Frenchman blood in his veins, also told me words that sounded like nothing I'd ever heard before, words his own mother whispered to him when he still slept in her arms.

Most can, I expect—mothers being mothers.

Nights, in bed, this is what I tell myself, saying the words only in my head.

"Fool," is what Dalton said. "Idiot," he shouted, slapping the loose leg of his pants. He would sic the dog on him, watching as he stumped thick-legged into the woods.

"Not mine," is what Dalton said.

Me, I went into the woods after my Mattie, chasing the shape of his broad back, calling off the dog that ran away the same day Dalton died. Mattie: shivering in dry ferns, hiding behind a tall tree, its shadow darkening his face. I held him, the bark pressing its pattern into my skin while he leaned his weight against me. That dog sniffed the ground.

"Shh," I whispered, patting my Mattie's back, "hush," I breathed, stroking the soft flannel of his shirt.

We waited for dark.

We did not move.

This—in summer, any summer it could have been, before Dalton, before Mattie.

I held to Mattie under arching trees. Leaves sifted slanting light.

What I heard in my head were the words he'd murmured the occasion he held me, like this, and the body's wordless answer, lifting, stretching, warming; taking in what is not its own—a time of year when cold did not give words shape, when water was not yet ice.

# HATTIE DALTON

The first sign we had was the sprinkler shedding lazy twists of water in a downpour. "We should take a look," my Penny said, pulling back the edge of the curtain. "No," I said, "she just forgot to shut off the faucet." After a few days of seeing water circle and fall, I went and turned the handle, then walked back across that soaked lawn, my feet squelching into what had become like a swamp. Grass grew tall that May, thick and green, and early dandelions went to seed. In a breeze all those gray puffs scattered. Forsythia and bittersweet, untrimmed, waved curled shoots before the windows Penny said stared at us like dark eyes. "I can see myself looking back at me when the sun's right," she told me.

Walking down the road, we saw her mailbox hanging open and empty except for bits of straw, as if a bluebird or a field mouse had taken it as a nest. I knew the mailman brought her no mail in his old Ford, just rattled past her house, his tires raising a cloud of dust that took a good few minutes to settle again. The flag on her box was never raised.

By August, the grass, shaggy and yellow, rattled in winds, like a long sigh that didn't stop, like how I imagined it felt to live by the sea, a constant murmur that could drive men mad. "I can't help but think about it," Penny said. "Hush," I said, "and mind your own." The apple tree out back dropped all its fruit, and in the stillness we heard it fall. Yellowjackets hovered above the grass. I imagined dozens of them crawling over the rotted fruit, their antennae waving as they ate and ate.

Frost touched the ground one night, ruining our late tomatoes, though it melted as soon as the sun climbed over the hills. Some men come to deliver split cordwood for winter was who found her. We heard them knocking on the door, saw them circle the house, wading through that waist-high grass, pressing their faces up to the panes with cupped hands. I gazed out our window and watched everything I'd suspected—watched that ambulance come, lights spinning, faint in the sunlight that burned grass dry and bled color from things, watched them carry it out, and recalled her the summer previous, standing where they now stood hefting it to their shoulders, recalled her faded housedress big in the sun, her skinny shape inside it like a shadow. I recalled her slapping mosquitoes on her arms, walking to the elm dead of the Dutch disease, where she stood for so long I couldn't ever figure, and don't know to this day, what exactly she was doing, or planning to do.

Penny hunkered down below the sash, clutching her elbows and shivering.

# THE PASSION
# OF ASA FITCH

A sa Fitch sits back into the deep drift of powdery
snow—a night and a day's worth, and still falling—feeling snow on his bare neck, inside his cuffs,
against the skin of his calf, and feeling too the feeling
that something about his foot, or his ankle, is not right:
bent, it seems disinclined to move. He stretches a hand
toward it, but his gut interferes. He sighs. Around him
is scattered the small armload of logs he was carrying:
ends of split wood stick up from where they've punched
and muddled the otherwise tidy snow. He looks up into
the blur of purling flakes, then coughs, and swivels as
best he can to see if anyone might be looking—has seen
his tumble—even though the nearest house is two miles
downhill.

The flabby wedge of skin between the waistband of his trousers and his now-untucked flannel shirt is going numb where snow has worked up under his jacket. His feet are, despite wool socks and insulated workboots, and excepting his ankle, which has begun to hurt, numb. His nose feels, quite clearly, numb—or, rather, does not feel. His ears: beginning to turn numb, especially the more he thinks of them. It's a numbing wind blowing the surface snow about his face, he reflects. He adds his bare hands to the numb side of the ledger, then cups them to his mouth and blows.

Asa can see his own deep and shapeless footprints behind him, down the slope to the barn, and in front of him the peeling clapboards of his house, the back stairs rising out of the snow. He tries to heave his weight forward to embark upon the process of standing up, but winces; now his ankle burns. Snow settles around him, making the faintest sound against itself.

The entire back hallway of his house is stacked floor to ceiling with at least a cord and a half of well-seasoned hardwood. Maybe pressing a few sticks into the crook of his arm was only an excuse to breathe the cold air, to walk knee deep in the new powder he's been window-watching all morning, to see if any tracks had disturbed it yet. Or maybe some part of him has covertly wished for such an outcome. A year ago, a car stalled amid an unplowed hood-high drift, and the driver, from New York, had—instead of wading down the road to the house half a mile away, where Millie O'Keefe swore to a reporter that her lights had been on until eleven thirty—kept the engine running for heat while snow drifted up around the tailpipe vainly trying to melt it. "He had cross-country skis strapped to the roof of his car!" the town cop said on the regional news broadcast the next day, his face red either with cold or excitement at a dead body, or both, the TV cameras registering quite clearly the snot frozen in the graying hairs of his moustache. A few years before that and a few villages upriver, at a New Year's Eve party, a high school boy sauced on Schnapps and vodka had stumbled outdoors in T-shirt and jeans to piss words into the snow and passed out; the other kids'd found him frozen some hours later, the yellow letters YOU FUC abating into a senseless squiggle, or so went the version of the story that didn't make the local weekly—"Not very good at his *pen*manship" was the punchline Asa tolerated more than once in the following week. ("You fuckers," Asa muttered in response: the kid, after all, had been right.) And during the worst wintry nights of his distant childhood, Asa had to endure his father telling and repeating the same old stories: the missing hunter they hadn't found until the spring thaw, when the snows retreated to reveal him still leaned against a rock, his shotgun beside him, drops of melted snow like tears on his preserved face; and the skier who, so hypothermic he'd believed he was warm, hung his coat on a branch and left twin tracks for the Forest Service to follow to his body the next day.

If pneumonia is, as his father'd often said, the old man's best friend—quicker and easier than so many of the alternatives—what better way to catch it than sitting numbly in a snowdrift? Asa often considers wandering off into the woods on a cold night, alone save for a bottle of brandy, but always concludes that he would rather enjoy congress with a woman one last time first. But, had he drunk more this morning, he thinks, he might muster something beyond a trickle and carve his own incoherent epitaph in the snow before expiring: SCREW TH GOVT!

He pushes back from his forehead the wool hat Lucy crocheted for him, scratches beneath its weave, and ponders his circumstance: twisted down in the snow, bum ankle, no feeling in anything else, rather out of breath from carrying the wood this far, and no one to ask for a hand up, if pride would permit him a posture lower than this one he presently occupies.

It is on numb hands and knees that, leaving the logs as they are, he proudly snowplows his way back into the house.

Asa is still exalted with the greater part of his hair, though what part remains sticks up from his liver-spotted scalp, he has to admit to himself, in a snowy derangement that resists water, comb, and the occasional patting of his hand. And these days there seems to be more hair tufting from his ears and nose than arrayed on his chest for a woman's hand to stroke. One evening Asa discovered himself trimming these hairs from his nostrils with a tiny pair of scissors he'd excavated from Lucy's sewing basket while humming "Bye Bye Blackbird," then caught his own eyes in the mirror and, letting his voice trail off on the lyric "No one here can love and understand me...," threw them aside rather than bother with such a nugatory effort—though his life, from his current prospect, seems a sort of tribute to the nugatory. He tends toward loosishness about his chin and jowls, but has somehow accomplished the preservation of the majority of his teeth. His nose is often slightly moist, and he is more likely to correct such humidity with deep yogic inhalations or the hem of his sleeve than with one of the boxes of tissues slowly acidifying since Lucy last plucked one. Whatever weight he's lost in his limbs has migrated to his stomach, where, during the hockey games he tunes the TV to, he caresses it like the ears of an old and faithful dog. He shaves with cold tapwater, and believes in the honesty of a cold toilet seat, which prevents lingering; he uses the hot-water faucet largely to dissolve the crystals of his instant coffee. Asa has one green eye and one blue eye, and has always felt that they offset any deficiency in his stature—he was once measured, sock-footed, at five foot seven and three quarters—to give him a certain advantage with ladies. Doesn't matter which one he winks. "Let me see that again," he imagines them saying. "Again." "You're awfully choice on those eyes of yours," Lucy told him, early in their marriage, after encountering him judging his three-quarters profile as he alternately blinked and leered at the bathroom mirror.

Throughout the rooms of his house, a faded pattern repeats itself on the walls. Cobwebs mantle the curtains and droop from the ceiling like crepe-paper streamers. Leaning stacks of newspapers now historic occupy much of the floor. In the living room's leftover room, near hearth and woodstove, a flimsy metal television tray with a selection of brown-ringed mugs and medicine bottles stands at the edge of an old braided rug gone clawed and tattery. At this late stage of things, he inhabits only his living room, kitchen, and pantry, sleeping and eating in the permanently reclined reclining chair from which he watches the television and the window, and leaving the upstairs for the mice and squirrels and the few of Lucy's cats—their names, save for an elderly orange tom that he calls Carl Yastrzemski, now forgotten—that remain to hunt them. The horsehair plaster behind his chair is dimpled and cavitied from all the times he's whacked it with a broom handle to end some in-wall ruckus. At the landing of the stairway the cats have in recent years scratched the wallpaper and plaster away to the laths, and sometimes he sees one jump up and vanish into that darkness.

Asa prefers burning wood to burning oil to heat his house—certainly he appreciates the scent of burning oak more than that of burning petroleum, but he owes his preference mostly to the work involved in keeping a home stocked with wood and keeping a fire hot, the forthright labor of axe and maul and wedge, of match and breath and kindling and fussy poker. For decades the wood and the fire were an empire entirely his own, but for some time now he's suffered well-intentioned interlopers. Each September, Asa stands by his window, half-behind a faded curtain, to watch Lon and Lee Hubbard dump a truckload of wood in his dooryard and then spend all afternoon splitting and stacking it in the back hall of his house. "Don't work any air into that pile," he calls from the doorway, more out of a puzzling obligation to play the jeezly old cuss than any belief that they would cheat him. "I want it nice and tight, or I'll whack you in the head with one of your wormy sticks." Lon drops his axe, spreads his feet, and raises his fists—"Come on, then, Mr. Fitch," he shouts, "I'll whack you back"—but Lee merely shakes his head. Later, after he has poured Lon and Lee shots from his bottle of McMaster's and with minimal eye contact they have all drunk and noted and commented on the meteorological conditions, Asa admires all this work done on his behalf, though the old Yankee in him—that is, all of him—blushes at such a sentiment, or is, mostly, too ashamed even to blush.

❄

Inside, Asa belly-flops into the kitchen, kicks the door shut with his good foot, and swoons on the floor. What he needs now, he thinks, his hands and feet beginning to throb, is a warming beverage, but how to reach the bottles atop the counter? It will be some time before Marnie arrives, and she won't sanction a sip, anyway. He looks up to where he left the bottles of brandy and whisky that his old friend Cy Littlejohn's son Sam, after cashing Asa's signed-over social security checks, brings for him every week or two, along with a few bags of groceries, now that Asa no longer drives. From above, an insouciant cat face peers at him over the edge of the counter. It is the roguish gray one that he is certain never belonged to Lucy. "I'll give you holy-old hell," he says in what he hopes is a sinister whisper. He shakes a fist and the cat shies back, then leaps to the top of the refrigerator, its hind legs scrabbling up. It hunkers in the shadows above the dusty coils and regards him from this new vantage.

This sight somehow inspires Asa to feats of exertion of which he did not know himself still capable. Head throbbing, he rolls onto his gut and does a half-hearted push-up until his ass is airborne and he can get his good leg under him, then struggles into a one-kneed crouch and hoists himself up to the counter where, dizzied and panting, he leans on both elbows for a moment. Here is the brandy. He decides he can forgo a glass, tucks the half-finished bottle under his arm, and stumps one-leggedly off to his broken recliner.

First he must tend the stove—the logs he put on before heading outside have crumbled into embers—and

turn on the television. His set predates the era of the remote control and the cable- or satellite-ready input jack,
and Asa, apart from enjoying carnal concupiscence with
a woman, most aspires to assume a weeklong recumbency
and switch among a hundred and fifty channels with an
infrared beam before succumbing. Depending on time of
day, weather, and whether one of the cats has knocked the
twin telescoped antennas out of his rigorously attained
alignment, he can receive between two and four stations,
though one of the two clearest signals is ricocheted down
through the mountains from Quebec, and except for this
channel's hockey broadcasts he understands none of it.
As an image wobbles into being on the dusty screen, he
settles into his chair and props his suffering foot on the
footrest. He hopes to find his favorite program, the one
in which, for example, two young women—of dishev-
eled habiliment, stringy hair, prodigious weight, odd
accents, and puffy and/or mottled skin—argue before
an unsympathetic lady judge about the precise division of
a seventy-three-dollar phone bill remaining from the five
months they spent cohabiting in some linoleum-floored
apartment. Are they lesbians? Asa wonders, trying to
conjure one of these women lying atop the other on a
bare mattress and stroking her swollen skin, or the two of
them kissing. He savors such mental images, and believes
them not too far from the truth: from the glimpses of the
outside world he catches through his TV, more and more
women seem to be enlisting with the other team every
day, and he also thinks he sees some of these women on
his rare trips down into the valley. If the lesbians have
infiltrated even these rocky, spruce-clad mountains—still
free of herbs-and-vitamins shops, liberal democrats,

and four-dollar cups of coffee—then the end times are indeed upon him.

But he has missed this program, and now an entirely different sort of woman—wearing her short hair in a flip against her thin neck, and dressed in a crisp cotton shirt—watches, wide-eyed and appreciative, a man in a chef's apron melt chocolate in a saucepan. Asa's too exhausted to get up and turn the dial, so he also watches this nonsense for a moment, trying without success to picture the host of this show—mature and severely made-up, yes, but still svelte—in her unmentionables. Even the commercial break, featuring a spot for some new shampoo, proves unhelpful: since when did kaleidoscopic images of grapefruit slices and strawberries replace a demurely naked-shouldered woman under a stream of water as the way to sell a bottle of perfumed goop? Finally he gives up and strains forward in his seat to peel down his wool sock. He suspects his ankle is broken, knows it is at least badly sprained, but wants to see the color of the bruise. He gropes his foot from the arch up to the knob of bone at his ankle, poking his flesh the way he imagines Dr. Hazen would, though Dr. Hazen would not be so gentle. Asa's pale and veiny skin has already turned a purply black. He touches it, and some part of him observes a wave of white light wash over the room. "Holy jeezum," he whispers, and eases back into the hollow his body has shaped in the chair. On the screen the sensible middle-aged woman licks chocolate from her finger and, he notices, winks at him.

"Let me see that again," he says, winking back. "Again."

❄

For six months now, Marnie, the new woman, has come every Tuesday and Friday. The other woman Dr. Hazen had ordered for him was called Christine, or Christie, or Chrissy, or something—Asa mumbled her name from his mouth as Christly, letting the *i* go short or long depending on his mood—but he'd managed to scare her off after only a month through such tactics as farting audibly in her presence and answering the front door in an uncinched bathrobe. He hadn't liked her plump fingers on his wrist when she took his pulse, or her loud lip-licking speeches about proper diet and nutrition, or the way she tried to corner him with the thermometer or the blood pressure cuff and bulb.

The great regret of Lucy's life, as she'd often liked to remind him, and the greatest joy of his own, as he'd occasionally reminded her, was that their monthly cubicular grapplings had failed to achieve even one of the expected brood of shiftless children, and though for years she'd begged him to talk to old Dr. Judson about this deprivation after her doctor had said it wasn't Lucy's fault, his own interpretation of masculine mores had absolutely forbidden him to do so. Now, blessedly, there was no one in the world to harass him into taking a room at the Old Folks' Home down in town, at least until Dr. Hazen followed through on his threat to declare Asa unfit to care for himself and sent the men in white coats to drag him away.

Billy Bowen, his oldest friend, ended up in the Home some years ago, after his hip gave out and his kids decided they couldn't afford to waste the already meager inheritance on a live-in nurse, and when Asa went to visit

Billy, he found him as far out of his head as a lumberjack a few hours after payday. Then Amos Thibault, on some government pension, checked himself into the Home and declared it a minor paradise—cranberry sauce three times a week, skittish young nurses to goose, a bedpan for when you didn't feel like standing up, and someone to clean it for you. Asa had walked out of the Home that time determined never to come back. Amos caught the flu the residents disseminated one winter and didn't see the spring, and though Billy's obituary has yet to appear in the paper, Asa's sure he too is long gone. Still, a year or two after Lucy's funeral, some of the busybody widows—the Beef Trust, he calls them—let it be known that old Ace Fitch was lingering on up alone in his house in the hills, and shortly thereafter Dr. Hazen began harassing him about what would happen when he slipped on the stairs in the middle of the night or the winds knocked out his power for a few days.

But Asa's passions are private. They require the range and remoteness of the hills. "Put me in the Home, put me in a pine box," he's told Dr. Hazen.

Dr. Hazen changed tactics then, harassing him about home health aides and Meals on Wheels and—"You do smell, ah, a little gamy, Ace"—bathing assistance. "What about a visiting nurse?" Dr. Hazen said. "Couple times a week. And someone else to bring lunch up for you."

Did they really provide sponge baths? He was scared to ask Dr. Hazen for fear the offer would be rescinded.

"Consider it a compromise," Dr. Hazen said.

Asa shrugged. "You're the doctor." He felt a smile lift at least a little of his cheeks.

He did not want Christly to touch him. And Marnie has not yet offered to give him a sponge bath, though

59

he has collected from the barn several old, not-unclean sponges he might once have used to wipe down machinery and left them lying about as signs of his willingness. As far as he's concerned, Marnie can tickle him with a wet sponge any time she likes. Her short and possibly lightened hair and her wool work shirts seem indications of potential lesbianism, but these days he's not sure if women are supposed to keep their hair short. He is a bit disappointed with her attire—before Christly came, he'd imagined the visiting nurses in starched white uniforms that would rustle in the quiet of his house, with white stockings and white shoes—but the look on her face perpetually warns him against saying what wants to rise to his lips. Usually he heeds it. He has decided, for starters, not to test the word "lesbian" in her presence. Asa likes to sniff the wake she leaves as she walks around his chair, affecting several long breaths to distinguish its bouquet—dish soap, hints of lilac perfume, something subtly spicy, all these lovely wafts of womanhood. He's wondered what in hell Marnie is short for, and once asked her, but she pretended she hadn't heard. Marnelline? Marnice? Marnelle? Marnanne? Because he lives too far up the dirt roads for the Meals on Wheels ladies to trust their delicate sedans, Marnie brings him dinner in foil-covered bowls she somehow keeps warm the ride out here; when she peels back the aluminum, steam rises, and Asa sees the trickle of condensation in the crumpled folds. From his cupboard she takes a plate and glass, and when he's eaten she runs water, and with her back to him washes up in silence.

"Good service here," he once observed.

"Only the best," Marnie said without turning around.

"Bet your husband appreciates your cooking," he essayed another time; scrubbing and splashing across the kitchen, she ignored him completely.

On the days Marnie doesn't bring him his supper, he prefers to hop into a half gallon of ice cream, or settle down with a family-size bag of potato chips. By the time the Bruins are skating off the ice for the first intermission, he's rummaging the bag's rumpled corners for the salty scraps, licking greasy potato dust off his fingers before drying them on the chair's upholstery. For breakfast, he takes his toast nearly burnt, his instant coffee black but for a splash of Canadian whisky, and, when he remembers, one of the Geritol tablets Dr. Hazen insists on.

The first time Marnie's car—new and small, some indescribable color not quite bronze, and likely foreign, from what he could tell through squinted eyes—appeared through the trees at the end of the pasture, he watched her gaze at the house and barn, the overgrown trees, the bent grass unmown and thick with seedlings, before she clipped the car door shut and set a casserole dish on its hood while she tugged off a pair of leather driving gloves. The weather had yet to turn cold, but she'd muffled her neck in a long scarf that trailed down one shoulder. Driving gloves? Already he liked this one. Maybe she could be persuaded to slap his bare bum with them. He watched her wade through the growth, stopping once to pick a burr from her sleeve.

"I suppose you're the person from home care," Asa said, holding his door wide.

He saw her eyes flick past him to the seventeen yellowing years of the *Herald* he hasn't yet had the heart to put in the burning barrel, the stacked Sears, Roebuck catalogs and ladies' magazines going back even farther, the colored medicine bottles along the sills, old boots and work gloves, three calendars each marking a different year, the hole the cats had clawed, the woodstove and soot-stained hearth, before returning, grudgingly, to him.

"My wife's," he said to her, sweeping an arm at the room behind him. He confirmed the corner of his mouth with his tongue. "Couldn't bear to throw anything away. Will you come in?"

She nodded, though the next week when she visited she asked if he wouldn't like to have some of the old things cleared out. "What if you get a cinder from your stove?" she asked him.

"Ahh," he said. "Hasn't burned down yet."

The television station has gone to the local news report, and tonight the dark-tressed Mediterranean beauty he thinks must be imported from New York City if not the old country itself does not gaze into the camera with her large liquid eyes and caress with her lips and tongue such phrases as "Authorities are investigating the possibility of arson" for Asa's delectation. At the left-hand side of the newsdesk, in her stead, a young man with ferocious jawline and fluffed hair stretches the shoulders of his suit and stutters. Asa, adrift on his recliner, watches a steady slant of snow over darkening woods and fields. Fenceposts split with age stagger across the pasture, each topped with a white dome. Perhaps the Christian Brothers, sipped immoderately, has burned some of the sensitivity from his tongue, because that organ too now seems rather numb, and he has quit talking to himself. But his ankle has returned to a state of absolute feeling that has him trembling unless he suckles from the bottle's narrow mouth. He swigs again.

This second bachelorhood has been so much more exciting than the first; it is a time of reckless musings and hypotheses and experiments and concomitant revelations. He has, through various empirical data, determined that he needs to change his trousers only every fortnight or so, though his underwear and socks must be freshened every third or fourth morning to avoid offending his own sensibilities. Until today, he last stepped outside and walked farther than an idling car back in September, when he wandered down to the edge of his land, near the razed swath the power lines cut on their way over the mountain, and listened to the crackle of electricity for a few minutes that warm afternoon—there was no other sound but the wind in the spruce—then unzipped his pants to piss on the base of one of the giant metal towers, wondering, as he did so, if his urine would conduct a twenty-thousand-volt shock up his tallywhacker. He survived. Now, given the opportunity to observe the effects of a damaged ankle on one's well-being and ambulatory capacities, he wishes he could find pencil and pad. Lucy's departure has allowed him the depths of dereliction he'd nearly forgotten during their long years of marriage, and, with this license, he's been contemplating a handlebar moustache and sideburns, or asking the boy at the new 7-Eleven downtown where he might find himself some of these dangerous designer drugs the Mediterranean newscaster is always mentioning, and how much cash he might have to bring along for the—is it?—score.

Asa tips the bottle to his mouth again, sets it down on the television tray, rearranges his weight in his seat, and considers the word "raunchy." He knows what it means, but wonders if there also exists something called raunch—some element or spice, some fruit or synthetic, that inspires one to feats of raunchiness? But the only dictionary in the house, could he even locate it, is an illustrated student volume, printed and bound in the latter days of the nineteenth century, that Lucy inherited from a maiden aunt who for nearly five decades taught grammar and composition at a girls' school in some frontier state such as Pennsylvania or Michigan, and from which, he is certain, the aunt long ago struck out all the baser vocabulary.

Whatever raunch influences Asa makes him want to touch the body of a woman. He does not believe it would be a struggle to rally himself for the moment, as some of the recent advertisements on the television suggest it might be for many men. No, he feels prepared—and not wholly unwilling—to assume at least some of the responsibilities that attend such an event: a long soak in the tub beforehand, a razor and a splash of Bay Rum, the purchase of gifts, a few diligent nods while she talks. For at least a part of each day, he itemizes those women whom he might touch, and every time discovers that Marnie heads this list, before the newscaster, if only because of her likelier availability.

But, in spite of such urges, Asa has no use for the senior socials down in the valley of which Dr. Hazen's encouraged him to avail himself: dances where neither partner can lift a leg an inch off the floor, games of cribbage and pinochle too boring for anyone to gamble or cheat, singing groups (hymns and show tunes), watercolor painting, competitive needlepoint, noncompetitive table tennis, bereavement circles. Somewhere around the living room he has the Old Folks' Home's tri-fold brochure with lists of such activities and cover photo of smiling, bespectacled, wheelchaired old-timer attended by smiling nurse and smiling grandchild. But the brochure, Asa knows, omits the ratio of biddies to fogeys. As a fairly cogent, non-drooling widower, he is part of a distinct minority and thus highly sought after. While a less discriminating gentleman might enjoy such a situation, Asa is chary of it: all those widows are either old, or fat, or old and fat. And all of them are desperate, turning their gazes in his direction so that the overhead fluorescence flashes off their eyeglasses at him, plucking at his sweater sleeve so he'll stay and listen as they tally their ailments and their grandchildren and great-grandchildren, and fussing over his hair if he so much as lets them. Leave them their creased pastel slacks, their orthopedic footwear, their unmuscled arms waving as they walk, bulging purses held out as ballast! He long ago decided he wouldn't disgrace himself by sitting in an overheated basement while kids serve him turkey and gravy and pop 'n' fresh rolls on tinfoil plates and a tinny stereo plays Glenn Miller and all the old, fat, and old and fat ladies bat mascara'd eyelashes at him.

Ellie Beckett's been the worst of the lot, ever since old Jack Beckett went a few summers ago. Asa made the mistake of accepting her moist and weepy hug at Jack's funeral and the Beef Trust has considered him sensitive and sweet ever since. Her false teeth don't fit dependably, though she exhibits them in an inspired smile whenever they meet, and then pesters Asa with counterfeit memories of his younger days in town in which she performs some conspicuous role. In her presence he keeps his eyes wide open so that he does not inadvertently wink at her. He believes her the sort of person to whom things are always only now occurring, and she wears this expression of startled wonder at all times. Some months back, Ellie had her grand-niece—about whom she frequently boasted, because the girl had spent a semester and a half at college in Connecticut before some crisis (impregnation, he guesses, or perhaps drugs or incipient lesbianism) returned her to work the night desk at the motel on Route 113—drive her up to Asa's door for a visit. He'd recognized Ellie's old car—Jack's old car, really—and crouched beneath the windowsill while Ellie knocked on the door and that grand-niece pressed her hands to her diseducated face and breathed on his windowpane. Though Ellie had opened his door a few inches and called his name into the mannishly fusty interior, she had not dared to find a path through Lucy's knee-deep newspapers, for which he could finally be grateful.

It seems too late for supper, so Asa gulps the last of the Christian Brothers and swirls it around his mouth before swallowing. He knows if Lucy were still here, she would have called Dr. Hazen hours ago and summoned one of the county's two new ambulances, which would've struggled through the snow to his dooryard so a team of burly guys could strap him to a board and bear him away. But he'd been against the taxes for the new ambulances and the new high school gymnasium, and didn't want to be conveyed in any vehicle he'd been extorted to pay for—never mind being carried by other men.

Anyway, tomorrow's Tuesday, and Marnie will be coming. He'll hitch a ride to town with her even if it means riding in that foreign car. The whole way down to the valley he'll feign indifference and look out the window, perhaps asking her about the new houses tucked into freshly cleared lots and the lawyers and orthodontists who own them. Then, maybe after he's outfitted with a new plaster cast or whatever other indignity Dr. Hazen decides to invent for him, he'll suggest to Marnie that, though she's been a guest in his house, he's never seen hers. When she invites him over, he can either seduce her, or, if she does indeed have a lesbian roommate, at least satisfy that part of his curiosity. Or maybe, he thinks, after their night together, when Marnie's in the kitchen the next morning making him oatmeal with raisins and brown sugar and a dab of butter, just a pinch of cinnamon and a pinch of salt, the way his mother used to serve it, he'll bump into her lesbian roommate on his way out of the shower. "Well," Marnie will say, "I suppose it's time I was honest with you both...."

The logs have burned to orange embers and the room turned cool, Asa realizes. The windows show only his reflection. He decides to get out of the recliner and see, on the way to the woodbin, how much snow has piled up. Using both hands, he lifts his foot from its perch, but the swell of blood in his ankle and foot seems to drain his faculties elsewhere. Holes appear at the edges of his vision and expand like burning paper. The foot itself is too tender to set on the floorboards. He clenches his teeth and hoists it back to the chair's worn upholstery.

"By the mighty," he gasps, wondering if this is what it feels like when you're about to pass out, and, if it is, whether Marnie will still allow herself to be seduced by an old man who faints over a bum ankle.

In a minute he has recovered enough to reach his right hand down beside the recliner, where this morning he dropped his bedding—one of Lucy's old afghans, a goosedown quilt, a wool blanket Lucy would've used only on a picnic, a pillow stained from the nightly impressions of his head. He draws these items up to him one at a time and, shifting and shivering, makes his nest. The woodstove ticks; the television's lambent strobe irradiates his home. Asa shuts his eyes and tries to think of stories for Marnie's visit tomorrow. She and Dr. Hazen are the only audience left to him, and Dr. Hazen is interested in listening to little besides his in and out breaths through the stethoscope. But they've given Marnie questions to ask—if he's warm enough, if he needs anything from town, if his appetite has improved. He does not reply "Be warmer with you over here next to me," "More hootch," and "My appetite for love?" and so, by the time he's produced the answers he believes she wants, she's usually washed the dinner dishes and slid her coat on.

"Ever tell you I once shot a two-hundred-fifty-pound buck?" he asked her one of the first times she came. "Twelve points. Dragged him out of the woods myself. Lucy made me slippers from his skin."

"Sound warm," she'd said. "Are those new pills giving you headaches?"

"Not as I'd notice." He heaved himself from the chair to get the door for her. "See you at the prom," he said, holding it wide and winking. "I'll be the one with the flower in my buttonhole."

Asa blinks and looks around the sunlit room, hearing the television's murmur and a wind against the sashes. The flue bangs. For the entirety of their marriage, Lucy would, each morning, bring him his coffee in bed, and on the coldest days he decides that this is what he most misses about her. Not the hot coffee, but the gesture—her having already faced the day he could not yet bring himself to. He rolls up in the recliner and considers his next move. By the program on television—a man and a woman sitting on stools and holding cups of coffee themselves—he knows Marnie's arrival is still hours away. Before she knocks on his door he must achieve at least an appearance of respectability and get the house warmed up again. In increments of inches, he scoots to the edge of the recliner, then shoves off.

The newspapers cushion him, to an extent, and he has several minutes to reflect on this disembarking tactic before he feels capable of crawling. But the woodbin is not far, nor the matches and kindling-barrel, and he has a fire lit by the next commercial break, when the hosts have begun to entertain a sullen and unshaven young man who, it appears, has been in the movies. Asa watches, but can't quite make out what the young man mumbles while the pucker-lipped hosts nod. "That whole situation's been overblown in the press," he thinks he hears.

He crawls across the frigid slate hearth and toward a frosted window prismatic in the morning sun. If he leans his elbows on the sill and kneels, he can remove most of the pressure from his ankle and still see through a corner of the pane: swirls of wind whisk surface snow from one drift to the next. Asa guesses a little over twelve inches has fallen, and, if this appraisal is accurate, then he cannot imagine how Marnie's foreign coupe will climb the slopes here: his road is low on the list of those deemed essential for the plows.

The telephone, mounted on the kitchen wall so that Lucy could clutch it in the crook of shoulder and neck and gossip while she cooked supper, but silent for several years, is, it seems, still operational: whatever jingle bells hide within the plastic cabinet suddenly resound through the room. Asa turns his head from the window in hallucinatory wonder when the telephone rings again, a strangely feminine chime in this place. He nearly expects to hear Lucy say, "Really? No! Oh, my. No," for a few minutes before coming into the room and asking him if he remembers old so-and-so and then repeating some story told already too many times. He's imagined the wire embedded in those tangled curls would have oxidized entirely by now, or the telephone company disconnected him—he can't recall paying a bill—or some new technology rendered this tiny machine a relic. When he and Lucy first moved here, there was no service this far from the valley, the treetops yet unblemished by poles and wires; a few years later, a party line stretched the length of the road; some years back, the doctors and real estate developers demanded their own private lines, and the telephone company capitulated. Before long, he imagines, there'll be curbside garbage collection and selectmen-sponsored weed abatement.

The telephone rings again. It must be Marnie, he thinks, and puts his hands back on the floor, scooting his good leg under him and dragging the bad one behind, bumping the recliner's stuck-out footrest, cobwebbing his nose, and snagging a splinter in his thumb. All the while the ringing continues, intervals in which he can hear the woman television-show host laughing merrily and blood whooshing through his eardrums. "I'm coming," he shouts, scaring Carl Yastrzemski into a bolt up the stairs.

By the hallway, his elbows and shoulders ache, and he pauses to rest. But the telephone insists, each metallic peal still startling him with its suddenness. He somehow flounders into the kitchen and collapses against the wall; the telephone is two feet beyond his reach. He tugs on the coiled wire, trying to swing the receiver free from its hook, then sees a frayed broom in the darkness under the kitchen table and crawls to retrieve it; with his failing strength he swings the bristled end at the receiver and, after several misses, knocks it to the floor. Before he can even reach it he hears a woman's voice, made trebly by the wire, speaking from the pinholed plastic. He reaches for the phone and slowly cradles it to his ear. "Hello?" he inquires. "Marnie?"

"Well, Asa Fitch, if you hadn't answered in a dozen more rings I was about to call the police to go check on you," the voice says. "Took you thirty-one rings to answer, did you know that? It's Ellie Beckett. How did you make out in the storm?"

Asa swallows and tries to catch his breath. He can, at least, safely blink. "Ellie?" he repeats. "I thought it was somebody else."

"Well, it's me," she says. "Who else would it be?"

"Oh, I don't know," Asa says. "Anyway, I'm fine. Made out fine."

"Down here the roads are a mess and the schools are canceled and there's no one out but the snowplows and some of us were sitting around and figured we'd better call people like you stuck up there in the hills." She pauses. "Course you're the only one still up there that we know of."

"It's fine up here," Asa says. "Just fine. Sun's already melting it."

"Do you have any supplies laid in? Medicines, food?"

"I'm fine," Asa says. "Just fine." He eyes the hook on the wall, assessing its distance and whether a well-placed toss of the receiver would seat it in the cradle.

"I hope so. Betty Parsons picked up a couple of day-old chocolate cakes at the Grand Union yesterday, so we're going to have a party later."

Asa grunts.

"Well, don't you be too stubborn to ask for help if you need any, Asa Fitch," Ellie says. "You call us if you need anything. We'll be thinking of you."

"That's nice of you to tell me," Asa says. "But I'm fine."

When the oversized black pickup truck—near saltless and mudless except for a few fresh streaks along its fenders and doors, and with fog lights and rollbar but no toolbox or gunrack or bed filled with raccoon-chewed plastic garbage bins bungee-corded together—crests the drifted road and pushes through the snow toward his front door, Asa is ready. He arranges his foot on the padded footrest, folds his arms behind his head, and listens for the thump of her steps on the front porch, the knock, and then, a minute later, the door's cautious swing inward and Marnie's voice calling "Hello?"

"Knew that little car of yours wouldn't make it," Asa crows. "That your husband's shiny truck?"

He watches Marnie step inside and shut the door behind her. She's wearing a lumpen, quilted coat, tall boots, and dungarees. She looks at him for a moment. "Borrowed it from a friend," she says. "What happened to you?"

"What do you mean?"

"The stove's not stoked up to five hundred degrees. Your face is white," she says. "Are you feeling okay?"

He cannot check himself. "Better, now that you're here!"

She unzips her coat. Asa watches her walk toward him and swallows hard. She takes his wrist, turns his hand, and presses her fingers against his vein. This unexpected come-on makes him buck, a bit, and that motion shocks his ankle into a new achievement of excruciation.

"You're panting," she observes. "Do you feel fever-ish?"

"Nope," he says through his teeth, regretting the missed flirtational opportunity but unable to muster any more detailed response.

She looks at her watch—all the dead-batteried and unwound clocks in the house show different times, like some international news bureau—and seems to concentrate. Asa too concentrates, on the profile of her slender nose and her fine-but-long and unembellished lashes. She could teach the Beef Trust a thing or two about makeup, he thinks: in the curtains' filtered noontime light, her beauty is supernal.

"Normal," she mutters. As she lets his wrist drop, she takes a step back, and the side of her thigh brushes his up-pointed foot: Asa hears his startled bleat before he knows his mouth has loosed it. "Ankle," he gasps as cover for his girlishness. "Twisted it. Maybe broke it. Yesterday afternoon."

"Jesus," she says. "Why didn't you call an ambu-lance?"

"Just want," Asa gasps, "my money."

"Oh, for God's sake. Where's your phone?"

"No," he says, reaching up toward her, though she's out of reach. "No. Not the ambulance. Please. I'll ride down with you to the doctor's. I promise."

She stands halfway between him and the house's further recesses, and he's about to continue his plea when she snorts. "Fine," she says. "But we're going now. Where's your coat?"

Marnie is able to lace up one of Asa's boots, though his injured foot, swollen and raw, remains stockinged after several attempts to ease it into the other boot. "You son of a whore!" he sputters, then adds, "My foot, I mean."

"I'm not carrying you out to the truck," Marnie says.

"Can I lean on you?" he asks, winking. "Your special friend won't mind, will he?"

She says nothing, but holds out her arm at its elbow. Gripping the recliner's armrest and the crook of her arm, he hauls himself up, and they lurch out the door. He squints against the wind and the knee-high midwinter sun, but, with his arm looped through Marnie's, can't adjust his collar. His nose begins to weep. Snow has feathered up onto the porch; snow, in fine showers, spirals down from the eaves; snow obscures the terrain between here and the truck. His foot, filled with blood again, aches and tingles.

"Ready?" Marnie asks. He tightens his grip on the quilted sleeve; she lowers one boot and knocks snow sideways to clear part of the step. "Okay?" she says. She takes another step and he follows, holding half his weight on Marnie, the other half on the rickety rail Lucy unsuccessfully nagged him to fix for at least a decade—well after the change of life, when she could no longer nag him about children. Scrape, shuffle, bow, wince: they gain another step, then another, and shamble on through the drifts, his stockinged foot carving a blurry trail through layers of snow. "Almost there," Marnie says, and then Asa feels his good foot slip forward and his weight start to follow. Marnie clutches at his coat. He shuts his eyes. Somehow they swing about together and he stumbles into her, one arm still caught in hers, the other over her shoulder, but both of them, now facing the house and its blown-open front door, still upright.

"I see you've been practicing your dance moves," he says.

"Every night for an hour," she says. "Are you okay?"

"Never better."

"Then let's get you in the truck."

They wobble toward the truck, where Asa sets both of his palms on the obsidian paint job like a suspect about to be cuffed in another of the television programs he enjoys. Marnie digs in her pocket, presses a button on a teardrop-shaped plastic gizmo, and the truck flashes and beeps. She opens the door. "Hop in," she says, extending her arm again. "I'll go damp down your stove and lock the door."

"No key," he says, holding the lip of the roof and stepping up to the chrome running bar one-footed. He climbs into the cab and settles himself with a grunt.

"Right back," Marnie says, shoving the door closed behind him.

The truck's vast interior still smells like new carpet. There are no old paper coffee cups or fast-food wrappers or socket wrenches on the floor. Asa watches Marnie walk back through the snow, then briefly checks the glovebox and side compartments for signs of a masculine or feminine presence. No cigarettes, one stiff foldout map of the state, an owner's manual (the lines for name and address on the last page left blank), no St. Christopher medallion, no AAA card, not even a candy bar or package of peanuts. He can't find the registration card, then sees a plastic sleeve with papers inside clipped to the sun visor on the driver's side. He leans over but can't get enough leverage to reach it.

Marnie has vanished inside the house. He has, on occasion, suspected that she steals his pills, and wonders if she's really damping down the stove—the chimney still huffs smoke. He has so many amber bottles on the kitchen counters, the windowsills, the bathroom, his TV tray—and why else would she drive six miles of poorly maintained gravel road up to his house twice each week if not to gulp a handful while serving him some warmed-over casserole? Still, she seems always awake without being what he'd call jumpy. Alert may be the word. Steady, she is steady, that Marnie. Marnifer? Marnitha? Dr. Hazen has offered him so many prescriptions he long ago forgot what any of them were supposed to fix, and wouldn't know if any were missing. Asa has a seven-compartment tray, each little bin marked for a day of the week, and there are even, he believes, some pills still inside it, though he has no idea anymore what they might be, or on what days long past he should have swallowed them. Several times he's sampled this buffet, and awakened hours later with its chalky remains at the corners of his mouth; because he so rarely enjoys such spoils, he's unsure what if anything in his pharmacy would appeal to Marnie. Some of the brown bottles were once Lucy's; some carry complicated multisyllabic names he could not imagine how to pronounce; some contain capsules that

expired during the last presidential administration; some
bear labels the sunlight has bleached blank.

When Marnie jerks open the driver's door, he pretends to stir and open his eyes. "You're back," he says.
"Thought I'd have to drive myself."

"Wouldn't get far without these," she says, cupping
the key ring in the palm of her driving glove. "Or do
you hotwire cars?" She twists the key and the V-8 engine
rumbles, then roars.

"Have," he says, though he's not entirely clear what
hotwire means. "That whole situation's been overblown
in the press," he adds, as she backs the truck and shifts
into drive.

"Ah," Marnie says.

Asa has almost never been driven by women: his
mother did not drive and could not imagine driving, and
he suffered the indignity of being driven by Lucy only
on rare, booze-blasted nights years ago. He plucks at his
seatbelt. "Can we get a little air in here?"

"Come on," she snorts, gesturing at a digital display
on the dashboard. "It's seventeen degrees outside."

"Well don't kill me on the way to the hospital," he
says. "The doctors can take care of that once I'm there."

"What are you talking about?" she says, looking at
him this time.

Asa slumps sideways toward the window. The tops of
bare, silver-barked trees quiver and bunch in the wind.
The truck's tires make no noise on the snow, and Asa
can hear the faint creak of Marnie's driving gloves as
she turns the steering wheel. In a moment they pass the
first driveway, which winds through the trees and over
a small rise to some new homesite where, he supposes,
a day trader with solar panels and electric heat stands

in his jockey shorts by a floor-to-ceiling window and complains over a long-distance line about how he can't get downhill for the snow. He shifts his aching ankle.

The last time Asa drove was some years ago and some pounds ago. Seven and twenty, respectively? He cannot be sure. That August, his worsted pickup truck still had the rusty plow attached, and he headed out for a long low stretch of dirt road that had flooded in all the spring rains and had since dried into a nice half mile of washboard. His plan was to help make his stomach a washboard without having to send a check or money order for $19.99 to obtain a piece of plastic and rubber advertised on the television in the hours after Lucy went to bed. He fitted his belly behind the wheel and set out, flesh jiggling, then dropped the plow on the hardened dirt and stepped the accelerator up to forty-five. If all that jarring didn't vibrate away his belly, nothing would. The noise was tremendous. Sparks sprayed. In the blur of rearview mirror he thought he saw metal parts spinning off into the goldenrod. This was good. At the end of the road he raised the plow, backed around in the weeds, and thought to give it another go. His gut already felt loosened. "Whew!" he shouted out the window.

This time, holding the knobbed steering wheel while his teeth tried to sever his tongue, he thought to look down at his gut—maybe he could watch himself reducing. And oh, the jeezless thing was jouncing and jelly-rolling. He whooped again, just as he looked up through the windshield at a fast-approaching tangle of branches and greenery. "Hold 'er, Ace!" he shouted as the wheel whipped through his hands. Plow and truck dipped into the ditch along the road, crashed through a thicket, and, slowly, tipped over sideways. The weight of his gut followed in the same general direction.

Cy and Sam Littlejohn towed him out, but the oil pan was busted and one axle broken, and anyway Lucy told him she was keeping the keys though he'd had only a bump on the side of the head and a bruised elbow. By the following summer, the truck had already been captured by bittersweet and poison ivy and now the growth has rendered it near as shapeless as he is. Lucy, to the last, never did tell him where she'd hidden the keys.

"Bad curve coming up," he says to Marnie.

"Thanks," she says. "But I've driven this road once or twice before. I know an old bastard who lives at the end of it."

This coquetry causes him to redden. Marnie takes the turn, sharper than he recalls, smoothly—not hitting the brakes and fishtailing, not going so slowly she loses all momentum in the powder. Asa eyes himself in the slightly frosted sideview mirror, and, because of either his flushed features or Marnie's aplomb, can think only of his shameful squeal and the folly of his planned seduction. He's wanted to be called a lascivious old coot, to behave cootishly and have someone snarl the term at him, but if circumstance and one serene, imperturbable visiting nurse have so discomfited him that he blushes like a schoolboy, his cooting days are, he thinks, over without ever really having begun. The wind blows plumes of snow from the branches.

They reach town more quickly than he expects, and here the asphalt has, despite Ellie Beckett's complaint, been cleared: huge banks line the sides of the street, the occasional car half-buried beneath. Asa looks at the row of storefronts along Main, and scattered between Brodeur's Hardware and the Agway and Twilley's Diner and the package store he sees one sign advertising USED DVD's and another that offers TROPICAL TANNING. Marnie does not appear to notice. She tugs a handle on the side of the steering column and squirts vivid blue liquid onto the windshield, then flicks on the wipers to clear it. In a moment she pulls the truck into the parking lot at the hospital and steers toward the doors marked Emergency, outside of which Asa sees a half-dozen young men—wearing EMT sweatshirts and sunglasses, hands either holding cigarettes or stuffed in pockets, crew-cut heads bare, laughing as they kick snow from their boots and mostly study the circle of pavement between them—standing beside an idling ambulance, its lights spinning in the sunshine.

Asa folds his hands atop the thin cotton johnny knotted behind his back so that the doctor working the ER today—a tall woman with ringleted hair and restless, oversized eyes—will, when she returns, hopefully fail to notice the stirring she causes in his barely girded loins. Marnie, after talking to several nurses and filling out some papers—"What do you mean, you don't have your Medicare card?" were the last words she spoke to him—has disappeared again, so Asa lies on the paper-covered gurney, his bum foot now splinted and propped on a pillow, and looks at the ceiling. He has already been forced to swallow several speckled tablets for pain, and been wheeled back from Radiology, where he was outfitted in a lead smock and made to lie down on a cold metal table. He feels almost comfortable enough to nod off, and, but for the frequent traffic past the open door of his cubicle and the garbled voices on the intercom, might do so.

Instead, he occupies himself reordering his list, and has just ranked the doctor between Marnie and the Mediterranean newscaster when she taps a knuckle on the jamb and without waiting for his say-so steps into the room, a stethoscope dangling like a necklace, pens poking from the pocket of her unbuttoned lab coat. "Well, Mr. Fitch," she says, flapping an X-ray in the air, "you're lucky. It looks like a clean break." She places the film against a light box on the wall and uncaps one of her pens. "Can you see this?" she asks, pointing the nib to the image.

"Sure, sure," he says, sitting up and squinting. He is looking at the ribbed turtleneck sweater beneath her lapels.

"Okay. You managed to fracture your fibula, just above the lateral malleolus, here. But the good news is your ligaments look fine, no tears, and everything in there is pretty stable. Sometimes you'll see a bone chip floating around, but you must drink a lot of milk." She smiles; Asa nods. "There's no real displacement. We're going to keep you overnight to let the swelling subside, and then get you fitted for a cast. Any questions?"

"Will I have to go to the Old Folks' Home?"

She laughs. "No, no. We'll send you home on crutches tomorrow if everything's okay. Do you have a ride? As long as you can manage around the house on crutches, or have someone come help you, you'll be fine. Wasn't that your daughter who came in with you? I'm sure she can help out until you're back on your feet again."

"Daughter?" Asa snorts. "Barely know her. I'm single and unattached," he says, winking.

The doctor smiles again and pats his hand. "Well, Mr. Fitch, I bet you'll be taking your girlfriends dancing soon. I'll call your primary care physician—Dr. Hazen, yes?—and arrange a follow-up appointment." She gathers her X-ray and clipboard, and pauses in the doorway. "A nurse will be in to check on you in a few minutes. If you're still feeling any pain, let her know and she'll bring you another pill."

Asa watches her sashay into the hall, and clamps his hands together more tightly. He leans back and closes his eyes; the paper rustles beneath him. His throat tickles. Down the hall, he hears a door latch, and the muffled sound of running water. A voice outside his door says "Knock-knock," as if beginning a bad joke, and a young, buxom nurse comes in holding a small paper cup and a can of ginger ale. "The doctor said your ankle was still sore?" she says. She overturns the cup into her palm and passes him another speckled pill, then cracks open the can of ginger ale and fills the cup halfway.

"What's this?"

"Just something for the pain." She seems almost to sing rather than speak. "Here you go."

Asa places the pill on his tongue and takes the fizzing cup from her. Swallows. Belches.

"I hear you're spending the night," the nurse says.

"I hope so," he says. "But this bed's awful narrow for the both of us." He winks.

Some time later, Asa thinks he hears Marnie talking to someone in the hallway outside his door. The intercom on the ceiling beeps once, then hums with static infernally faint. It seems that Marnie is explaining to someone—the doctor, he realizes—that she has to leave him and go home because her lesbian roommate will be getting worried about her truck. But he can't quite make out the words above the buzzing. "What?" he says. "Wait—I'm in here."

"Don't I know it," says a different nurse, dressed in what appear to him to be pajamas—a baggy shirt and loose pants, in a matching pale green color. "We're getting a room set up for you, and then you can go back to sleep. How's your ankle feeling?"

Asa nods his head on the pillow and the nurse's face slides sideways and out of his vision. The gurney, oddly unanchored, seems to spin on soft currents of air blowing from the vents in the baseboards. Some vast, delicate weight—a heap of feathers, an armoire's worth of lingerie—rests atop his chest. His fingers and toes tingle.

When he opens his eyes again, a man in a down jacket is sitting before a window, haloed in diffuse gray light. "How are you feeling, Ace?" says the man.

"Dr. Hazen?" Asa says. His mouth feels pasty, his tongue swollen.

"I just stopped by on my way home. Heard you were here. Had a fall in the snow, eh? Can't do anything in this town without someone finding out."

"Guess not," Asa says.

"Well, they'll take good care of you here. And you've even got the room to yourself tonight, it looks like. How're you feeling?"

"A little dizzy," Asa confesses.

"Probably just the Vicodin," Dr. Hazen says. "How's the ankle?"

"Okay."

"Listen, Ace," Dr. Hazen says. Already the light fades in the window behind him. "I know we've talked about it before, and I don't want to kick you when you're down, but maybe it's time to think about moving to town."

"The Old Folks' Home?" Asa whispers.

"Your home health aide gave me a call this afternoon. Said you seemed to be having some trouble keeping on top of things at home—the housecleaning and whatnot," Dr. Hazen continues.

"What does she know," Asa says. "She just wants to take my pills."

"I can't tell you what to do, and I don't want to try," Dr. Hazen says. "There are other options besides the, ah, Old Folks' Home. Just think about it. How will you be able to get around on crutches for the next two months?" He stands up, holding in his hands a pompommed toque. "They'll be putting the cast on you tomorrow," he says, and fits the toque onto his head. "Just think about it." He waits another minute, lips parted as if to speak, then waves. "Have to go finish shoveling out," he says. "Been here since six this morning."

The indignity Asa feared suffering in hospital is, it turns out, even worse than he could have imagined: he does not need to pee into a cup, or have a thermometer shoehorned up his bum, but when, the next afternoon, the plaster splint is cut away from his ankle, the fiberglass cast that replaces it is purple.

"Most people prefer it," the doctor, an unshaven young man, tells him. "Doesn't get dirty, like plaster. And the fiberglass is lightweight."

"Purple's for little girls," Asa says. "How am I supposed to go on a date wearing this ridiculous thing?"

The doctor rubs his chin. "Maybe some women will like it?" he suggests.

After the doctor leaves, Asa lies under the blankets, watching the television suspended from the ceiling—he has a remote in his hand, and twenty-some channels to flip among, though the experience does not thrill him as much as he believed it would, and he watches the local news at noon, waiting for the lady judge to come on. If, after all, this is as exciting as cable TV gets, he supposes he may as well take that bottle of whisky into the woods. Otherwise, Asa can divine his future as Dr. Hazen and the Beef Trust—and Marnie, too, apparently—would have it: a home health aide is but the first in a series of irrevocabilities. Soon he'll look forward to the daily arrival of the Daybreak Adult Daycare van to take him to the Old Folks' Home for coffee hour and card games, pill-feedings and needle-proddings. He'll end up sitting in a ring of folding chairs in some overheated lounge at the Old Folks' Home while a stocky young animal shelter worker moves from resident to resident, letting each tap a palsied hand atop the mangy skull of an equally unwanted mutt on temporary reprieve from its steel cage, or participating in memory circles—here his imagination fails him—or having to stomach all those turkey suppers Amos Thibault raved about, the chemicals they inject in the dark meat making him as far out of his head as Billy Bowen. And forget about a drop to drink.

On the television, a husband and wife stand behind an oak podium and complain about another woman's birdfeeders. "I'm supposed to control what trees the birds fly to?" the woman demands. But before the lady judge can pronounce her verdict, Asa hears another knock at his half-open door.

"Asa Fitch!" a tremulous voice says. "Said he was fine!"

Asa turns to see Ellie Beckett push the door wide. Behind her, at either shoulder, are Betty Parsons and another old and fat lady he thinks might be Dottie Dalrymple after a few years of eating day-old chocolate cakes. "They're just about to decide the case," he says, pointing at the TV.

"Well hello to you too," Ellie says. "How can you even see that up there? You'll get a crick in your neck." She totters into one of the vinyl-covered chairs and snugs her sweater around her shoulders. "Cold in here!" she huffs. "Now what's this about your ankle?"

Betty and the large one scrape chairs close to the bed and sit down. Asa can hear the three of them breathing as they fix him with their gazes. "It's fine," he says. "Would've been fine on my own but my cleaning girl said I had to come here."

"Backwoods medicine," the large one says. "Just take an axe and chop it off if it gets infected." She wheezes out several low chuckles.

"Dr. Hazen told us you were here and would love some visitors," Ellie says. "We would've brought flowers but the florist didn't get their delivery yesterday on account of the snow, and all they had left were some old roses and a bunch of Shasta daisies and bluebells."

"Forty dollars for a basket of daisies," Betty says. "Can you imagine?"

"Might as well just all get our hair done for that," the large one mutters. "Basket of daisies."

"Good fences make good neighbors," the judge is saying, but Asa can't quite hear her. The married couple looks smug. He reaches for the remote, but Ellie is closer.

"Good idea," she says, picking the thing up and aiming it expertly at the set. The picture winks out. "Now we can hear each other better."

Asa turns toward her. Her teeth seem, today, a tighter fit, or perhaps she's grown into them. She has tied a gauzy silk scarf around her neck and, he notices, applied lipstick and eyeshadow. She smiles, her eyes watery and large behind her glasses. He coughs and sputters and feels his face and ears grow warm. A nurse squeaks past the doorway on rubber-soled sneakers. The large one pinches at her pantlegs, shifts in her seat, and says, "Oof."

"Well let's see your cast," Betty says. "I think I have a pen in my purse. We can all sign it."

"Oh," Asa says, "I don't know. I think the doctor said it had to set a bit more first. He wanted me to keep it covered. Out of the sunlight."

"I've never heard of that before," Ellie says. "You shouldn't be embarrassed. It's only a broken ankle." She turns to Betty and the large one and lowers her voice. "He said he was fine when I called him on the phone yesterday."

Asa watches the other women nod slowly. "Looks fine to me," the large one says. Her tongue peeks through her teeth while she chuckles.

The hospital has provided Asa with a pair of crutches and a four-footed aluminum cane quite different than the curved wooden one that, ever since Lucy dropped a cast-iron skillet on his big toe one morning two decades past—deliberately, he always insisted, whenever the subject came up—has made cameo appearances on damp days. He grips the cane's rubber handle and, through the lobby's tinted floor-to-ceiling glass, watches Sam Littlejohn pull up in his truck to drive him home.

"Here he is," Asa says to the nurse reading a magazine at the nearby desk, then rocks back and forth in his seat to gather momentum to lift himself upright. He picks up the crutches one at a time, fits them under his arms, and stumps forward into the hospital's electronically revolving door, each chamber large enough for a corps of wheelchair-riders, though the machinery spins so slowly that Asa can hobble through. The discharge nurse, her breath scented of some artificially flavored bubblegum, comes up behind him carrying the abandoned cane. "Can you manage all right?" she says. Asa, grunting, declines to answer. At the curb she and Sam both hoist him into Sam's truck.

"Throw this in the back?" Sam asks him, holding the cane beside the window.

"I don't want that goddamned thing," Asa says. He hears it clatter in the bed. Sam gets in and cranks the ignition.

"Feeling better?" Sam asks, and pulls out of the parking lot. Asa says nothing. They drive downstreet, and Sam pulls up beside a snowbank in front of the package store and leaves the engine running. "Hang tight a minute," he tells Asa. The skies are overcast again, and from them a few flakes fall weakly. Asa watches them alight on the windshield, tiny crystals collapsing into water drops.

Sam returns with two paper sacks, which he hands, clinking, to Asa so he can shuck the cellophane from a pack of cigarettes. "One for you and one for me," he says, jerking the gear into drive and stomping on the gas pedal. Crumpled waxpaper and styrofoam cups tumble across Asa's feet, and a cigarette lighter slides across the dashboard and smacks the passenger window.

"Ahhh," Sam says. He punches in the lighter button next to the radio and pulls a Marlboro from the pack with his lips.

They cruise past the edge of town. Asa notices snow-covered dirtpiles from scraped-over fields and the raw plywood frame of a long low building that he missed yesterday. Plastic tarps stapled unevenly to its roof flap and billow; through square holes cut in its sides, in which windows will be installed, he can see a line of bare trees. Where the muddy snow before it meets the road, a crow pecks at a snarled lump of squirrel carcass. A bit farther, a signboard standing in a roadside clearing announces the future home of Valley Self Storage. He turns back to Sam, who smokes silently, steering one-handed as he slows for the turn to take them back up into the hills.

"How much is a cup of coffee?" Asa asks him.

"Cup of coffee?" Sam says, looking at him, then back at the road as he spins the wheel. "I don't know. Maybe a buck fifty at the gas station or the 7-Eleven, seventy-five cents at Twilley's."

"Not four dollars?"

"Not that I know of. You fancy or something?"

Asa waves his hand. "Ever see any lesbians in town?" he asks.

Sam coughs out smoke. "This isn't Massachusetts," he says.

Asa looks back out the window: more birches and spruce; low, layered clouds. The road climbs, and the wet asphalt yields to snow. He appeals to Sam's profile. "I think I'm in love."

"Love?" Sam snorts again, pumps down his window, flicks his butt onto the road, and rolls the window back up. "Sounds more like desperation, with all this talk about lesbians. You know how much a sex-change operation costs?"

"Ah, blow it out your ass."

Sam looks through the windshield for a moment, then says, "Love, huh?"

"But she doesn't know it."

"You afraid to tell her?"

"No, I told her. Tell her all the time. She just thinks I'm kidding."

"Is this one of the gals the nurse told me were in to see you this morning?"

"One of them?"

"Hmm." Sam nods slowly a few times. "Not your type." He coughs. "Guess it's been a while, eh?"

"Don't you bring her into it!" Asa says, then lowers his voice and adds, "God rest her soul."

"I need another cigarette," Sam mutters, reaching for the pack.

Asa slouches. The truck bounces and squeaks on its shot suspension. "Don't you have any advice? You're young, you know about love."

Sam lights his cigarette with the dashboard plug's glowing coils and sucks at it for a long moment. "Don't ask *me*," he says, breathing out smoke. He turns on the radio and jabs the tuning button. Static oscillates into low whistles and subtones as they pass beneath the lawyers' and orthodontists' telephone wires and the electric transformers mounted to the utility poles. "Jesus, I don't know," Sam says, switching the radio off. "Get her drunk?"

❄

The agonies of the flesh—and, between the four daily in-gestions of the Tylenol with Codeine No. 3 the ringletted doctor has prescribed him, his ankle torments him—are nothing, Asa realizes, compared to the agonies of love, al-though, in his present circumstance, they seem conjoined. Now that he has confessed his secret, if only to Sam Littlejohn, he is unsure whether this love is something he should deny himself—through fasting, silent solitude, further mortification of his wasting anatomy—or a final opportunity for his wilted spirit. Is this love mere raunch, or is it some absolute and irreproachable feeling? Asa knows only that he has not been privileged to feel such pleasurable distress since the early days of his marriage to Lucy. His hands tremble with it.

He eats a packet of saltines he took from a tray at the hospital, swallows his evening painkiller with sips of Christian Brothers and, feeling warm and itchy, passes out. The next day, as he watches some soap opera in his recliner, Asa's eyes sting with tears, and he even sobs once or twice over the young blonde woman lying pale in a hospital bed, who, he gathers, was pregnant but lost her unborn baby and husband in a car crash several episodes back. Injured herself, she still has not awoken, but moans and flutters her long, thick eyelashes while her family and friends circle the bed.

Lucy would, every few months, petition him to take her to visit her parents, who lived in a cramped house two hours' drive into Maine. Before one such trip, Lucy—so she let him know—had been up since four in the morning, baking bran muffins and icing a cake she'd taken from the oven the night before, while he'd slept on until five thirty; they were on the road by six o'clock, so that Asa could frustrate his father-in-law's efforts to deride him for rising late. The night before, a late October rain had stripped the remaining leaves from the trees, and when they walked to the car, Lucy carrying the covered cake plate and muffin pan, and he their overnight luggage, the predawn sky was still overcast. Sometime on the road east Lucy fell asleep, one hand still atop the carefully balanced cake. Her head lolled on the seat and, as he alternated glances between her face—he still thought it beautiful, as yet unlined with worry and distress from putting up with him—and the narrow road ahead, the early sun broke through the clouds and lighted her brow. He looked back to the twist of asphalt: the car was passing through a grove of tall pines still soaked from the evening rain, and, as the sun struck their bark, they began to steam, wisps rising up in shafts of golden light. He can remember nothing about the visit to his in-laws, only his wife, sleeping and beautiful and uncomplaining, on the seat beside him, while he steered his car through the hills.

The midday newscaster—too prim and fussy, as far as he's concerned, with a schoolteacher's enunciation and hollow cheeks—comes on to tell him about a house fire caused by an old space heater, a snowmobile fatality, and, a few towns north, a baked bean supper fundraiser for a new police cruiser. He watches an advertisement for a low-calorie canned soup and another for fingernail strengthener, then shuts his eyes—every time he takes a Tylenol 3, all he wants to do is sleep—but thinks he hears the weatherman saying "...rain through tomorrow, with some flooding in the valleys, so be careful out there on the roads." When he looks at the set, a different soap opera has come on. He lurches up on his crutches and blunders toward the window.

Indeed, rain falls over the pasture, packing the snow to a few inches of heavy slush from which emerge last year's burst milkweed pods, dead grass stalks, goldenrod shriveled black. Scraps of fog, fouled in old barbed wire and tangled hedge, hang. An ice storm, a decade or more back, brought down trees and blacked out the electricity from Lake Champlain to Lake Parmachenee, but otherwise Asa can remember no precipitation at this time of year but snow. This rain, he thinks, must be evidence of the global warming he's heard the Mediterranean newscaster mention a few times, and soon the ice caps will melt and his hilltop become a tiny island. Never mind the lesbians and the expensive coffee, the tanning booths and self-storage: the weather, it seems, is harbinger enough of the end times, impetus enough to act.

He doubts Marnie will come tomorrow—Friday, her usual day—given that she abandoned him in the hospital; she and her lesbian roommate have, most likely, already found more interesting bedfellows than a weepy and abashed old man. Perhaps even now she and Dr. Hazen are arranging for another visiting nurse to take her place. But this affliction of love needs a vessel more felicitous than some substitute Marnie or a soap-opera actress. If accessibility is his list's main criterion, he must reorder it. He dodders back to his recliner, and, with the rubber tip of his crutch, pokes the stacked papers beside it until they topple sideways, then roots among them until he finds the Old Folks' Home's brochure. He fits the crutch in his armpit and hops into the kitchen, where he hauls a dusty, cane-bottomed chair, the weave of which seems to have sustained some minor explosion, near the wall: the brochure lists a telephone number, and he hooks a finger into the plastic rotary and dials it now.

A woman's voice answers. "Mountain View Eldercare. How may I help you?"

"Hello, dear. I'm calling for Ellie Beckett, please," he says.

"I can connect you, sir," the woman says. "Just a minute, please." Asa hears an odd beep, and then someone else picks up the line.

"Hello?"

"Ellie? It's Asa. Hello."

"Asa Fitch? Well isn't this a pleasant surprise," she says. "How are you feeling?"

"Oh, fine," Asa says. His throat tightens and he needs to cough. "The doctor gave me some pills to take."

"Good," Ellie says. "That must help."

"Yes. It does."

"Good," Ellie says.

Asa does cough, into the mouthpiece of the telephone.

"Well I hope you didn't catch a cold in the hospital," Ellie natters. "Every time I go in there I leave sicker than I came."

"Oh?" Asa says, and coughs again. He takes a shallow breath.

"Some rain, isn't it?" Ellie says. "The weatherman said it was very strange to go from snow to all this rain in just a few days this time of year."

"Yes," Asa sputters, "very strange."

"Personally I won't mind if the rain just washes away all the snow. I'm not much of one for winter."

"Oh," Asa says. He waits for something else to come. Only a silence does. "Well, I just thought I'd call to say hello," he finishes.

"That's nice of you," Ellie says. "You know, there's a

song circle here tomorrow night, in the activities room. The high school music teacher is going to play our requests on the piano and we're going to serve coffee and donuts. Why don't you come?"

"Downtown?" Asa says.

"If you can't find a ride, I understand. I just thought you could join us. I remember you had a good voice. You can sit in a chair all night if your ankle's bothering you. Anyway, it starts at six thirty."

"Oh," Asa says. "Well, I'll see."

"I'll hope to see you there," Ellic says.

Asa hangs the telephone on the hook and hacks into his fist, thinking. Most of his wardrobe remains in the bedroom closet upstairs, untouched and possibly moth-eaten, mouse-nested, cat-clawed, or disintegrated at this point, even if he could limp upstairs on the crutches to verify that the red shirt Lucy bought him twenty years ago because, she said, it suited his complexion, and which he wore on their twice-yearly dinners out, as well as to the odd party to which they were invited, no longer buttons over his gut. He considers calling Sam Littlejohn to beg a ride to the men's store, but Sam delivers his provisions about once a week, never at the same time or on the same day, and Asa doesn't know his number: the nurse looked it up in the telephone book when he told her how to spell Sam's name, but if Lucy kept any telephone books about the place they likely date to Sam's teenage years. He needs some pomade for his cowlicks, and to locate that bottle of Bay Rum after all. Should he wrap some plain bandages around his purple cast to disguise its color? Should he bring breath mints? A bottle of wine? A forty-dollar basket of daisies?

In the living room, he verifies the improbable tick of rain wind-driven against clapboards and windows, dumps a log into the woodstove, turns on the television, then founders into his recliner and shakes a Tylenol 3 into his palm. This weather's not helping his ankle any, he thinks; better take another. He unscrews the cap of his brandy.

Asa wakes to Carl Yastrzemski licking his eyelids. He looses a last, arrested snore, feels raspy tongue and whisker-tickle, sees the half-shut, beatific eyes, and realizes that his open mouth is partly draped with a matted tail that's been dragged the length of the county. He curses and knocks the cat sideways off his chest, and wipes fur from his dry tongue with his hand.

Gray light fills the room. A gusty rain still falls. It might be eight in the morning or one in the afternoon; the even clouds affirm nothing. His head feels more addled and cottony than, on rousing, he's come to expect, but with nominal groaning he rises from his recliner and, crutched, bustles to the bathroom to prepare for the trip to town. He can't get his cast wet, so instead of filling the bathtub he offers himself the brief exemption of running both the hot and cold faucets and, cupping his hands, gathers water from each to splash over his head. One of the sponges from the barn sits atop the toilet tank, and he wets it to scrub his cheeks and behind his ears. His armpits—he tucks his nose inside his collar and sniffs—seem passable. There is still the matter of what to wear; hanging from a towel rod are several flannel shirts on wire hangers, and he chooses one of these that may have been recently laundered. His trousers and undershorts are folded on the dining room table that even Lucy stopped insisting they eat at once the television stations increased their broadcast wattage twenty years ago.

"One of my favorites?" he asks his reflection. "Well, I've been known to sing 'Bye Bye Blackbird,'" he says, and then croons "Pack up all my care and woe, here I go, singing low..." before wondering how, after all, he'll manage to get downtown. Given all the stockbrokers and dentists who've moved to the hills, there may be a taxi service, he thinks, but then realizes that these people will have private chauffeurs. There is, could he abide the enforced conversations with other old-timers, the Daybreak Adult Daycare van. With cup and brush, he lathers his stubble while he considers. Asa has been rotating among a selection of disposable plastic razors he bought, a dozen in a bag, last year or the year before, and he picks through them to find the sharpest one. He draws it down his jaw.

"Where somebody waits for me, sugar's sweet," he murmurs, leaning into the mirror and stroking the razor up his throat, "so is she."

He rinses the blade in the sink, and then pauses: he hears footsteps on his porch, a knuckle tapping the door, and then Marnie's voice—Marnie's voice!—calls hello. His pulse surges; he rushes to shave the last bit of bristle from his cheek, nicks a fold of skin, and watches blood bloom there. He dabs a scrap of toilet paper to his jowl. "Coming," he calls, sing-songing the word. "I'm just getting into my tuxedo."

"Well don't dilly-dally," she says. "I've got lunch here for you."

He thumps down the hall to the living room. "Lunch?" he asks. "Make mine a ham and cheese with tomato soup. Anyway, isn't it a little early for you?" She stands, dripping onto the newspapers and floorboards, two feet inside the door. Today she wears a baseball cap without logo, its brim and crown soaked; her short hair is tucked back so that it curls behind her ears and beneath the cap, and the humidity, he notices, has given it a bit of frizz. Her raincoat is of the sort, he thinks, one might purchase on mark-down at the Agway, though on her it is somehow enchanting. She holds a covered plate.

"It's eleven thirty," she says.

"Whatever you say, dear," he says.

She takes off her coat and hangs it carefully on the doorknob, but keeps her cap on. "I came up now because of the rain," she says. "I don't have the truck today and I want to get home before dark in case the roads get bad."

"Special friend's out in the truck, eh?" Asa says. The fathoms of his renewed feeling surprise him; now, regardless of special friend or lesbian roommate or date with Ellie, he cannot cease the stupid smile he feels creeping over his face. The agonies of love are, perhaps, only the agonies of separation. The agonies of the flesh—false teeth, osteoporotic bones, nearsightedness, obesity—he decides he can, as of this moment, no longer settle for.

"Something like that," Marnie says. "Do you want to eat this, or not?"

"Of course," Asa says. "I never turn down a home-cooked meal made with love."

Marnie shakes her head and walks past him into the kitchen. Propped on his crutches, he swivels and follows her. By the time he's arranged himself in his chair, she's presented him with a partitioned plate harboring a mound of mashed potatoes, a spill of wrinkled peas, and some sort of chicken cutlet. "Here you go," she says. "With lots of love."

He smiles up at her; he enjoys this game, too, but won't be taken unawares this time. "I didn't know if you were going to come today or not," he says, impaling, with his fork tines, several peas. "The way you left me in the hospital."

She leans back against the counter and crosses her arms. "Who do you think took care of everything?" she asks. "Someone had to fill out all the paperwork."

"Thanks," he says. "Probably be getting emergency room bills for the rest of my life."

She snorts; he carves at his cutlet. But she has not taken off her cap, and he still can't figure the design of her flirting.

"Anyway," he says, "I was thinking maybe you could give me another ride downtown."

"Today? How will you get back?"

"Call up Sam again. I'm sure he's not doing much."

She seems to consider this a moment. "What's downtown?"

He carefully arranges some mashed potato on his fork and affects dispassion. "Oh," he says, "some song and dance routine at the Old Folks' Home. Dr. Hazen said I should participate." He exaggerates each syllable of this last word, then shoves the potato into his mouth.

"Did he?" she asks. "I told him I think you should, too. Can't stay shut in up here all the time."

"So you'll take me?"

She looks at her watch; its metal band, he notices, is thick enough to be that of a man's watch. "If you can be ready in the next half-hour."

"Of course," he says, shoving another forkful of

potatoes into his mouth. He bolts the rest of his food, then crosses his cutlery atop the plate and pushes back his chair. "I'll go finish getting gussied up," he says.

In the bathroom, he winks at his reflection, peels off the blood-dotted tissue, and ponders his fortune: whatever mistakes he made with Marnie last time have been forgotten or forgiven, and now their romance will happen as he prophesied it. He wets his comb again and attempts to part his hair.

Asa watches the heel of Marnie's boot sink into the slushy mud beyond his porch steps, and eases one crutch tip onto the ground, then his good foot. The earth itself seems unbalanced, treacherous. Rain pelts his face and runs down his neck. Down the slope, the trees bow and reel in the wind. Marnie opens the car door for him and, shoulders hunched, waits for him to maneuver across his dooryard—who else, he thinks, would, on his behalf, loiter amid the bizarre fury of a winter hurricane?

"Like the end of the world," he says, trying to crouch to fit himself into her preposterous foreign coupe. She shoves his crutches into the tiny back seat, then gets in herself and starts the car.

"Never seen weather like this," he says, looking through the rain-smeared windshield.

"It's just two fronts coming together," she says. "Temperature's supposed to drop twenty-five degrees overnight, and the winds come in behind it. It'll feel like winter again tomorrow."

Despite its size and apparent flimsiness, her car, he observes, is a stick shift, and Marnie gooses the clutch and gas so the car doesn't slide in the muck. He sits in a leathery scoop of a seat, nearly on top of her—only the gearshift and emergency brake divide them, and, when she shifts, her hand brushes his knee. She clicks on the defogger and switches the blower to its highest setting. Asa is still uncertain how he's going to explain that, in fact, he has no interest in going to the Old Folks' Home to sing old show tunes, but will gladly squire Marnie to her house—although, he thinks, these faint but deliberate collisions between her driving glove and the outer edge of his kneecap may mean that such talk is unnecessary.

She feathers the brakes as they begin to descend. "You know you can downshift going down the hill, right?" Asa asks. "To slow us down? If you need to?"

"Don't start," she says. "You wanted a ride."

The coupe's wipers chafe back and forth to an even cadence. "So," he says. "You never told me what Marnie is short for."

"It's not a nickname," she says. She doesn't take her eyes from the branch-littered road.

"Oh, sure," he says. "What is it really? Marnalena? Marna?"

"Marnie. Now can I just drive?"

"Whatever you want, dear," he says, looking out the side window at the swaying trees.

The road, at this elevation, seems to have suffered no traffic beyond a perfunctory plowing and Marnie's and Sam Littlejohn's comings and goings to his house, Asa notices. But, farther down the hillside, the puddled mud, frozen and thawed and soaked again, has been tracked deeply with the oversized tires of the architects' and surgeons' sport utility vehicles—a piss-poor term, Asa thinks, for a truck. Marnie's car sways in these ruts, and mud slaps up inside the wheel wells and spatters the side window as she turns the steering wheel in her gloved hands.

"Do those really give you a better grip?" Asa asks. "Like in the Formula One races?"

Marnie says nothing. The car fishtails out of a furrow and slews across the mud before the tires find friction with the road again.

"You know mud's more slippery than snow, right?" Asa says. "Usually, more cars get stuck up here during mud season than in the winter. I think it was a few years back when a school bus got stuck in a muddy washout, and then the tow truck that went to haul it out got stuck too, and—"

They enter the sharp curve in the road, and, this time, Asa sees, Marnie steers the coupe too wide. The car sinks into twin ruts, rocks violently sideways, then yaws up, out: the rear half of the car floats away, Marnie wrests the wheel one way and then the other, something crunches against something else. When Asa opens his eyes, he looks through the windshield at treetops and rainy sky. The car, nose up, has sunk in the roadside ditch; the engine has stalled and, beside him, Marnie cranks the key.

"Jesus!" she shouts. "Fuck!" The engine revs on, and she punches the gas. The wheels whine as they sink deeper into mud, and then the car skids, slowly, backward, and comes to rest against a stand of birch. She shuts off the engine and ratchets up the emergency brake.

"Wow," Asa exclaims in that sudden hush. "Are you still in one piece?"

"Shut up," Marnie screams, banging both hands against the steering wheel. "You and your goddamned rides!" She covers her face with her driving gloves. "How the fuck am I going to pay my deductible?"

When, years back, before her sole passions involved nagging or otherwise expressing her various deprivations, Lucy would occasionally allow herself a fit of tears and wailing, Asa would decamp for the other end of the house or the outdoors until he deemed it safe to attempt to correct whatever damage he had, inadvertently or not, wrought. Now, he pulls his seatbelt, but, at the odd incline at which he sits, can't find the buckle to release it. He can, at least, appreciate Marnie's language. Rain smacks the coupe's insubstantial roof, and Asa supposes it miraculous that the two of them haven't been crushed. He waits what seems an appropriate interval, then clears his throat. "Well," he says, "someone will be by soon and haul us out. Those trucks the business executives all drive have lots of towing capacity, if you believe the ads on TV."

She doesn't say anything or turn toward him.

"Happens a lot up here," he offers, "this time of year. Be out in a tick."

Marnie sniffs, wipes her face, and leans her head back. As he watches her, it occurs to him that this is entirely a ruse for his benefit. For a woman, she drove skillfully in the snow, and certainly took this turn as if she intended to get the car stuck in the ditch—some variation of the old running out of gas routine, he thinks, which he himself practiced more than once on the dates of his distant first bachelorhood. This pageant of feminine emotion and excessive cursing seems so unlike her as to be staged, the sort of thing Lucy would have affected to make him pay attention to her again. His passion begins to rally and he has to clear his throat again.

"Marnalena," he whispers. "Is it all right if I call you that?"

Her face, turned toward him, is, if flushed and a little moist-eyed, composed.

Asa reaches past the gearshift to place his trembly hand on her thigh, and feels, beneath the denim, a certain warmth that transcends the foreign coupe's defogger. He allows himself a gentle yet firm squeeze of her flesh. For an impossibly long second, she looks at him with a boundless sorrow in her eyes, then lowers her gaze to his hand, her leg. He too looks at this strange geometry between them, the angles between his blotchy fingers and her leg a problem he cannot solve. Slowly, her hand reaches for his, and his raring heart rattles, but she peels away each of his fingers and replaces his hand on his own wrinkled trouser leg and the wasted muscles it covers. She shakes her head from side to side.

"Asa Fitch!" she says, omitting the middle name— Benjamin—his mother would have employed for such impudence.

So, he thinks, this is going to be more difficult than he anticipated. He looks out the windshield at the oddly canted landscape, then reaches for her shoulder, winks his green eye, pulls her suddenly toward him, and kisses her on the lips—which, he discovers, are neither soft nor delicate, as he has long imagined them, but somewhat dry and chapped.

Something hard strikes his jaw and he almost bites his tongue. He opens his eyes to see her gloved fist poised for another blow. "Don't you dare," she says.

He massages his face. "I thought you liked me," he says. "I've told you I love you."

Marnie thrashes in her seat until she can unfasten her seatbelt, then shoulders open her door. "I'm going to go get help," she says, stumbling out. "Stay here."

"Hey," he says. "I'm participating, like you said. Right? I love you, Marnalena."

She kicks the door shut. Asa watches her struggle up the muddy shoulder—her feet carve gashes in the slope, her hands sink up to her wrists as she clambers to the top of the embankment. Her cap askew, her short hair slick with rainwater, she reminds him of one of those women in the proper kind of shampoo commercial—the kind after which he feels pleasantly stemmy. She wipes her hands on her blue jeans and tugs her cap on tightly, then turns to walk down the road. He scrabbles at the window, but there's no lever to roll it down, only several buttons with icons he can't see clearly. "Wait," he shouts, "wait! Don't leave me here! I have a date at the Old Folks' Home!" He can't tell whether she hears; she's already out of his sight.

In the car's close interior, his breathing sounds loud and ragged, but after a minute he hears little but the ticking of the engine as it cools. The tilt of the seat is not unlike that of his recliner. A squall of wind and rain batters the coupe, but, for now, he's warm. Those orthodontists work long days, he guesses, so unless Marnie either finds one at home or walks all the way to town, it will be a long wait for a tow, assuming anyone can see the front bumper of the car sticking up from the ditch. The last Tylenol 3 he took is wearing off, and he craves another. Some Christian Brothers and potato chips. On the dashboard, a digital clock reads 12:18. He doubts he'll make it to town by six thirty, but, when he does arrive at the Old Folks' Home, he'll have a story to tell Ellie Beckett, about how his cleaning lady tried to kidnap him as a love slave, and maybe that'll at least make Ellie a little jealous.

# THE LIGHTHOUSE
# KEEPER

THE LIGHTHOUSE. Rising from the end of a narrow, rocky peninsula, the lighthouse commands a wide view of the ocean and the channel leading into the bay. It is constructed of interlocking granite blocks—designed to withstand high winds and surf—and rises four stories from the bluffs. Atop the tower, the lantern gallery houses the whale-oil-powered Fresnel lens shipped from France, which refracts the lamplight with a thousand pieces of glass. This lighthouse, unlike many, is square rather than round. On each story one window opens on a different direction, and these different views, the lighthouse keeper often thinks, give each room a unique character. The ground-level window looks north, toward land; the second-story window faces west, across the bay and the blinking lights of the channel markers, the ringing bells of the buoys; and the third- and fourth-story windows face south and east, toward the open waters of the ocean, from which ships arrive to navigate the dangerous shoals outside the channel's mouth, and into which these same ships, loaded or unloaded, soon disappear, quickly becoming dark blurs on the waves to anyone watching their progress.

THE ORIGINAL LIGHTHOUSE. Few people now recall, or are old enough to recall the stories about it passed down by grandfathers until the children stopped listening, the original lighthouse which once stood where the current lighthouse now stands. Built before the Revolution, it was made of wood and burned to the ground several years later. Another, second lighthouse may have stood between the time the wooden lighthouse burned and the time the present lighthouse was erected, but if so, no one remembers it except as a rumor—their memories and the old stories fixed instead on the fire, the beacon visible all night along the coast.

A ROMANTIC. The lighthouse keeper is, of course, a romantic: watching every day the roll of wave against rock, the drifting fogs, the endless gray sea. Standing in the glass-enclosed lantern gallery on the top of the lighthouse, he thinks of the eroding land, the action of the sea to reclaim what once came from it. On this coast, he knows every cove, every outcropping, yet the coast will change many times even during his own life.

BEACHCOMBING. Many sorts of objects wash ashore— dashed on the rocks below the lighthouse, entangled in the dune grass and birds' nests of the saltmarsh, abandoned on the beaches by receding tides. After a storm, driftwood and other oddments litter the sand. A pedestrian striding along the dunes may sometimes notice a figure on the flats, clad in shapeless garments, gathering whatever the seas have given. A bottle, turned opaque from years in the water, may have drifted from a wharf in Portugal or been tossed overboard from a ship in the middle of the Atlantic; or the bottle may have contained lemonade or ginger beer, handed to a careless child by one of the pushcart vendors who sell lunch to the summer crowds at the nearby beach.

POLITICS. The position of lighthouse keeper is politically appointed, though the lighthouse keeper forgets this at times. It seems to him that he has kept the light for years, and memories of his own life before he came to the lighthouse are hazy: mere scenes, with no action or explanation, are often all he can recall. The position may have come to him as it comes to many others—because of his status as a retired sailor, or as a gift from an old friend now in the administration. To the lighthouse keeper, plugging leaky casks of whale oil, or replacing a broken glass lamp chimney, it does not matter. Politics are of little interest to him, having nothing to do with his own duties at the light.

ROADS. A narrow road leads north from the lighthouse, following the coast, and arrives after some four or five miles at a small town square overlooking the channel, from which more roads diverge. One continues north and west along the channel toward the shipping port at the end of the bay; others, less traveled, lead east to the ocean and the mansions that overlook it, or to the beaches where in winter the only visitors are gulls and terns or Canada Geese flying south.

THE TOWN. From the town square, the view to the west, toward the water, is of gray-shingled houses, chimneys, and the swaying masts of docked boats. The town's fishermen wake long before the sun to navigate the channel and head for the offshore banks of haddock and cod, and return in the afternoon to sell the fish at market. Other townspeople work at the shipping port, as clerks or copyists at trading companies, or as longshoremen, unloading strange cargoes which may have come thousands of miles. Nothing of this foreign climate do they take home with them at night, or else it dissipates along the road between the port and the town, catching in the ragged branches of trees or blown away by the winds. At night, the town turns dark and quiet; most people go to bed with the sun and so miss the circling light in the tower at the end of the channel, winking at the slumbering town every few seconds. Only a handful of people in town—the insomniacs, the drunks who stumble onto empty streets late at night, the idle who do not rise to work each morning—see this flash of light in the dark, and, pausing for a moment, follow its beam out to sea.

THE BOY. In town lives a slightly built boy whom the lighthouse keeper pays to deliver sundries from the general store. The boy owns a bicycle fitted with a wire basket, or perhaps a small wagon with which he pulls behind him the goods the lighthouse keeper has requested that week. Candles, a pair of bootlaces, several tins of biscuits, a box of nails. People in the town square notice the boy—taking not only such everyday items but also wrapped parcels from the clerk at the general store and counting out coins not his own—and often speculate as to the contents of the parcels, as well as the nature of the relationship between this boy and the lighthouse keeper whom they seldom if ever see. It is known among the townspeople that the boy's father drowned one night in the channel, but the townspeople do not know why the boy does not work on another fishing boat as most boys do. The townspeople often see the woman they believe is the boy's mother walking along the road to or from the shipping port, where, they assume, she keeps a position of some sort to support herself and her son, though she never speaks to travelers she meets along the road, looking instead at the ruts of wagon wheels. But in the post office the boy pockets bundles of mail addressed to the lighthouse keeper, and when the door closes behind him the townspeople gossip.

A PARTIAL LIST OF SHIPS. Despite the presence of the lighthouse, many ships have been wrecked off the rocky point at the entrance to the bay, their hulls tearing open on underwater shoals. A partial list of ships lost includes the *C. H. Loughlin,* the *Magpie,* the *Edward P. Tarn,* the *Catherine Davis,* the *Shooting Star,* and most recently the steamer *Emily*—of which the crew, clinging to the wreckage, was rescued by fishermen, though not before several sailors had drowned, the bodies later drifting to shore with the flotsam from the hold.

THICKETS. On the point of land where the lighthouse sits, no trees grow in the winds constant from season to season. The ground is covered with rock and patchy

grass, though just beyond the lighthouse, along the road
to town, many bushes thrive—sumac, wild roses, beach
plums, bayberry, junipers. The winds have carved these
plants into twisted shapes, and, uncut by any hand, the
stalks grow wild and dense, making thickets taller than
a man. The boy, on his weekly journeys to the lighthouse
and back, prefers to leave early, for at night the branches
cast tangled shadows, and behind him the light flares
every few seconds, showing each time his own shadow,
long and distorted in the instant he sees it, before him
on the road.

RELIGION. A small church, led by a pastor and a sexton,
serves the town. Its steeple is modest, but its whitewashed clapboard sides stand out among the weathered
shingles of the other local buildings. The pastor presides
over baptisms, marriages, and funerals, and bestows the
blessings of God upon the new boats built in town. On
Sundays, most of the townspeople assemble in the rough
pews for services, offering mumbled prayers and pennies
for the poor, listening to the pastor's voice as he reads
from gospel stories and psalms, though often all that
they may remember of these stories is a single word or
sentence—driven into the mind at the same moment a
fly alights on a hand, heard while trying to suppress a
cough, or summoning to memory a past conversation.

THE HOUSE IN THE DUNES. In places, the dunes between
the lighthouse and town rise fifty feet high, the rattling
rough-edged grass the only thing keeping the sand from
collapsing into the sea. Little-used paths wind through
the dunes, now climbing to a ridge offering a prospect
of the sea, now hidden from sight in a hollow. No one

recalls who made these trails or for what purpose. Some in town might surmise that the paths were originally used to scout ships approaching the channel—during times of war, perhaps, or by pirates. Now the paths are used by transients, or hunters, or else not at all. Yet in one of the low places along the trail, a small house has been forgotten, obscured each passing year by sand drifts which block the door and settle in piles across warped floorboards. Inside are no signs of former occupancy save some shards of broken crockery and ashes on the hearth, and only mice move within the sagging roof and defeated walls.

THE BLACKBIRD. The boy's friends have heard that the lighthouse keeper has in the lighthouse a caged blackbird which he has trained to speak and which whistles like a teakettle whenever anyone approaches the door. The boy describes for his friends the dull beak of the bird, rattling the wicker bars of its cage, and the glittering eye it fixes on him while he unloads the goods he has brought from town. The lighthouse keeper, the boy says, feeds the blackbird seeds, scraps of fat, and fish heads from his fingers, and while it eats the blackbird flaps its wings inside the cage, and feathers float to the floor.

NIGHTS. Alone nights in the lighthouse, the lighthouse keeper checks the kerosene font and leans on the lantern gallery's railing. He watches the sweep of the beam across scrub growth on the peninsula, sometimes wondering if the sudden movements he thinks he sees are real or only tricks of his eyes in the alternating darkness and light. On nights like these the lighthouse keeper recollects a feeling he first felt years ago: a winter night, when, in the quiet of the parlor, in the yellow glow of lamplight and the warmth of the hearth, he read Jules Verne's *Journey to the Center of the Earth*. That night, objects he saw daily became unfamiliar; shadows bloomed in the corners of the room; and outside the windows the night was quiet and icy cold. He remembers the sound of water rushing behind a tunnel wall, thirst, a beach littered with bones.

TO AVOID CONFUSION. Because of the great number of lighthouses, lightships, and lighted buoys along the coast, and the number of new lights constructed with each passing year, many lights are indistinguishable from one another; and the captain of a trade vessel returning from the Far East may easily mistake the light at one port for the light at a nearby port and so run aground, losing the cargo he has brought from some distant harbor. Prominent lighthouses are then modified with different characteristics—some with twin towers, others with fixed lights instead of revolving ones, and still others with colored glass in the lens—and the changes published months in advance of any alteration. But still, at night in severe weather, the multitude of lights, red and white, blinking and motionless, seems as profuse as the stars and planets to a sailor suspended in his ship's rigging, trying after many long months to determine his home port.

CHORES. Always to be done: trimming the wick, filling the kerosene font, polishing the brass, cleaning the lens, upkeep of the tower, whitewashing and grounds maintenance, winding the bell, studying the sky and winds for fog, hoisting the weather pennants on a pole. Or: untangling fishing nets, caulking planks, patching sails, planing boards, checking lobster traps, coiling ropes. Or else: mending worn clothes, darning socks, stirring chowder, sweeping wooden floors, tending the fire, scouring cookware.

AN INFIRMITY. The boy does not tell his friends that the lighthouse keeper has the use of only one hand. The lighthouse keeper has not described the accident that deprived him of his hand nor even made mention of the infirmity; but the boy cannot help but notice that when he collects his weekly pay or when the lighthouse keeper gives him coins to purchase goods, he uses only his right hand, awkwardly opening his purse and letting the coins fall to the table, where he sorts among them. What remains of the lighthouse keeper's left hand is swathed in cloth or hidden inside his shirtsleeve. Only kind of work he's fit for, the boy thinks, as he walks home along the darkening road, fingering the few coins in his pocket.

THE PASTOR. To the townspeople the pastor of the church is a reassuring if distant figure. Though they seldom ask him for anything, he seems always to know when help is needed, and is quite discreet about dispensing aid to the indigent. The pastor believes in preserving an individual's pride in a town such as this, where everyone knows everyone else, and where sooner or later anyone may need help of some sort. Yet when the pastor comes to town, the parishioners who on Sunday greet him with courteous words avert their eyes, believing, perhaps, that as he knows when someone is in need, so he knows when someone has sinned.

BOOKS AND STORIES. Lighting a small lamp on his table, the lighthouse keeper slowly unwraps the parcels the boy has delivered, or uses a pocket knife to cut the coarse twine binding them. Inside are leather-bound volumes he has purchased from book dealers in Boston and Providence. The lighthouse keeper treasures most those moments in his day when the morning's chores have been done and there is time to eat his dinner and study a book before commencing with the afternoon's activities. Again, at night, while above him the light turns on its revolving table and he hears no sounds save the waves and distant buoys, he lights the lamp by his nightstand and reads, cradling his book against him with his hand. More than anything the lighthouse keeper hopes someday to come across the story which he remembers hearing as a child, spoken in his mother's voice while he sat curled in her lap. He remembers a strand of his mother's hair brushing his cheek as she read. The rain outside the window, the gentle motion of the rocking chair. The sound of pages turning. He cannot recall the details of this story, nor any of its events or characters, but feels certain that should he discover it again he will recognize it at once. And so he orders more and more books, which already fill shelves on the second- and third-story chambers of the lighthouse, and spends his time away from tending the light in reading.

GHOSTS. The boy, like many people in town, believes in the presence of ghosts, the spirits of those who have died terrible deaths and must linger near the sites where they left their bodies. Haunting what they think still belongs to them, the boy's father once said, years ago, though now he has been dead three winters. His boat was found capsized in the middle of the channel one evening, and his body was never recovered. For a time the boy's mother believed that her husband was not dead but lost, abducted, or amnesiac—perhaps having received a blow to the head and then rescued, but unable to speak his own name to those who had delivered him from the sea—and she traveled each day to the shipping port, riding in a carriage when one was available, walking when one was not. There, the boy believes, she spent the daylight hours searching for her lost husband, hoping the sight of her face would stir his memories. Exhausted, she returned each night, past dark, and retired to her room without speaking. The boy blew out the candles he had kept burning for her. Then, in the darkness, he would creep out of the house and through the town to the piers along the channel. Lately his mother has ended her travels to the shipping port, yet at night the boy still slips from the house. His feet knock on the warped boards of the docks. Boats creak in their moorings. He listens to the splash of waves against hulls, smells the rot under the piers where at low tide seaweed and crabs have been left behind by receding seas. He waits always for a voice to rise from the waves, and though he does not know what this voice will sound like, choked with salt water, fragments of mussel shells, and the delicate bones of fish, he feels certain that he will recognize it when he hears it, the voice of his father gone these three years.

CHILDHOOD IN MAINE. Potatoes, the lighthouse keeper thinks when he thinks of his youth, fields of brown dirt, potatoes like rocks in ground only weeks away from freezing, gray skies, wooden barrels, numbed fingers, burlap, a line of dark trees, a horse-drawn cart, the horse's frozen breath, tiny flakes of snow falling over the children gathered in the field for harvest.

A HUMBLE DWELLING. The house where the boy lives stands on a plot of land between the town square and the docks, near many other houses like it: small, one story, wooden shingles grayed by salt air. The boy's mother once kept the wavy glass of the windows polished and the cramped rooms swept, everything clean and tidy if a bit worn, though now she stays in bed most days, and her son goes to market and prepares the chowder they eat for supper, peeling potatoes and cleaning fish. Now soot from the stove darkens the windows, and dust covers the curtains. Yet no one notices, no one stands by the window to wait for anyone's arrival, for the only person coming and going in the house is the boy.

A SYMBOL. In summer, when tourists arrive along the coast to reclaim the beach houses they have abandoned for the winter and to partake of the healthy seaside air, the lighthouse keeper often looks from his first-story window or stops a moment in whitewashing the fence to see a solitary person walking along the road from town. The person stands near the edge of the cliffs, watching waves churn over the rocks below, studying fishing boats moving along the channel, and especially gazing at the lighthouse, shielding her eyes with one hand as she squints at the revolving light. For these people, the lighthouse keeper believes, who come only alone and often at dusk on summer nights, the lighthouse means something: there is nothing else to draw them to this isolated point of land. It may be the lighthouse's dual function, perhaps—warning the sailors of danger yet also welcoming them at long last to shore with a beam visible some twenty-one miles—or else a connection to their own pasts: a lighthouse visited in childhood, the moan of a foghorn at the start of a long journey, the rhythmic sound of waves and the rhythmic motion of light.

VISIONS. The boy also does not tell his friends about the trances that lately have possessed him, those passing moments where the world before him blurs and another scene appears before his eyes, or when he finds himself in bed, unsure if he has been asleep and dreaming or simply lying awake. When he regains his sight he finds himself breathless, as though some pressure has been constricting his chest. Always the memory of what he has seen fades at once, so that he can recall only scattered images. Hands opening before him. Trees waving in wind. His father's face, asleep.

RAIN. In times of rain the lighthouse keeper feels most at home, mornings when sea and sky merge, indistinct, when few boats move along the channel and those that do seem possessed of a vague lethargy. The rain seems to muffle every sound but its own; the foghorn and buoys and steam-whistles of ships sound farther away than on clear days when from the lantern gallery he can perceive ships at a great distance. In times of rain nothing is clear. Clouds lower themselves to earth, water streaks the glass of the lantern gallery and the windows of the tower, and the ringing bells seem to come from another time, conjuring as they do so many other rainy days the lighthouse keeper has seen.

ECONOMY. The boy does not realize that the money his mother keeps stashed beneath the mattress she lies upon at all hours runs low. His mother has never worked, despite the guesses of the townspeople, and the family was never prosperous even when the boy's father fished six days of every seven. Now the few coins the boy has earned from his errands to and from the lighthouse, all of which he gives to his mother, are nearly gone. The boy's mother believes that her son spends his days working on the fishing boat of some local man, for he is often absent from the house, yet she wonders at the small wage he receives. Now, when he leaves, she searches through cupboards, in old jars, beneath loose floorboards for the money she imagines the boy has hidden from her.

THE TAVERN. The town's fishermen gather in a one-room tavern not far from the water, furnished with low tables, a darkened bar, and a haze of pipe smoke. Early in the evening, the last light of the sun fading from the grimy windows, the fishermen drink and swap tales, clustered in groups around one or another man with the gift of storytelling. The bartender folds his arms across his chest, overhearing several conversations at once, perhaps, yet dubious of all. For in the tavern he has heard many stories, and professes his disdain for those which he has not witnessed himself, or those in which truth and invention seem to blur, the storyteller perhaps repeating what he has heard and adding his own distinctions, so that each story leads out of the one preceding it and flows into the next.

STEALTH. After he has carried supper on a tray to his mother, and helped her swallow some broth, or a slice of bread, and after he has snuffed out the candles and the lamp, the boy steals quietly from the house. In town, few windows show any light. A dog may bark, or a tree groan in the wind, but the boy grows bolder each night, as his senses become accustomed to the darkness. Some nights the boy waits by the water, skipping stones into the channel to stir the silent voice of his father, and other nights he strays down the road to the lighthouse, carrying a stick in his hand. His ears fill with the rushing of wind. He does not know why he chooses this road, or why in fact he leaves the house at night, except that sometimes wind and darkness soothe him, and at other times rouse in him such excitement that he shouts wordless sounds at the trees and bright stars. In town, the friends who once sought him out for his stories of the lighthouse keeper and the caged blackbird now avoid him, ducking around the corners of buildings when they see him coming, and the boy does not follow them. In the darkness he desires no company. He cracks his stick against tree trunks and swings it through the air. Ahead, at the edge of land, the light winks at him. If the night is clear, the tower shines in the moon's glow. As the boy draws closer, he steps from the road into the thickets of bayberry and juniper, vaguely troubled by the expanse of landscape and the brilliance of the light, though no longer by his own solitude.

A CERTAIN PHRASE. In a small volume printed in England the lighthouse keeper comes across a certain phrase in his afternoon reading, and through the long hours of labor that night this phrase repeats itself over and over in his mind as he had repeated it earlier aloud, over and over, drawing his finger under the words each time he spoke them: *and beneath the trees a bower, stirr'd not by breath of air nor trill of water.* All the words that he had read until finding this passage fade from his memory until the slim book contains for him only this phrase, of which he cannot determine the real significance.

A LETTER. At the end of the week, the boy follows one morning the road he has taken to traveling by darkness, and delivers the mail to the lighthouse. Once he has left the town square and started on his road, where in the day people are few, and only a woman doing wash or a horse standing behind a fence may notice him, he examines the different letters which do not belong to him and which soon will pass from his hand. The postmarks often bear the names of Boston and Providence, or sometimes New Bedford, or, perhaps, of other places which the boy does not know and has never heard spoken. The business to which these letters pertain does not interest the boy, but only the names invoking the distant places themselves, towns and cities larger than this one, filled with brick houses and tall buildings and the noise of many people active at once. The boy longs to see such a place, though he feels that he cannot leave his mother, nor the voice of his father, speaking in the darkness with no one to answer it. The boy knows how a life may change with a knock at the door, remembering the night his mother pushed past the fisherman who had come to the house, running to the shore where she leapt into the channel and had to be restrained by the other men gathered around her husband's empty boat, but he does not think of this as he lifts his hand to the door of the lighthouse, and hears behind it the teakettle whistle of the blackbird as he raps on the wood.

TIDES. The advance and retreat of the seas is impercep-
tible to anyone watching. Each new swell may reach a
bit further up the shore as the tide rolls in, but it is only
when one has not moved for some time and suddenly
finds one's feet wet that the approaching tide becomes
remarkable.

GOVERNMENT. All democratic governments are, of
course, subject to the judgments of voters, and those
voted into office may find themselves quickly replaced
by others whom the voters have chosen. In town, few of
the fishermen vote; in the tavern, the preferred talk is of
sailing-ships and stormy seas and not of representatives
and legislation. Yet in the shipping port just to the west
and north of the town, merchants and owners of trade
ships all vote, selecting those candidates who promise
fewer restrictions on commerce, lower tariffs on goods. In
the isolated town, a man rowing a skiff along the channel
at dawn may not know of elections come and gone. Or
perhaps he has heard of them but has not found time
to cast his own ballot. Other men, sleeping in doorways
of the shipping port at this same hour, may know of
elections only because of the new coins in their pockets,
or the drink warming their guts—the price offered for
a vote for the candidate chosen by a wealthy merchant,
whose agent watched these men step into the booth and
passed them a small purse on their way out.

ANOTHER LETTER. In the light of the lamp, past mid-
night, the lighthouse keeper sits at his desk to write a
letter, stopping periodically to squeeze the bridge of his
nose with his fingers and thumb: *I have been a seaman
since my boyhood, and very much enjoy my situation here at*

*the light. I shall be very sorry to be removed, for I am a man of little means. Because I have function in but one hand, I will be hard set to support myself. I consider myself but a servant to your Excellency, and should be most grateful should you reconsider, for I attend to my duties with great diligence and believe I keep a good light.* The lighthouse keeper writes the words slowly, and the scratching of the quill on the paper and his own steady breathing are the only sounds in the room. When he finishes the letter he clutches the lamp in the crook of his arm and a stick of sealing wax in his fingers, allowing liquid wax to drip on the folded paper. The lighthouse keeper extinguishes the lamp and in darkness climbs the stairs to the lantern gallery to trim the charred end from the wick. It is late, and though he is not tired he knows he must sleep, and wait, and do nothing but tend the light. It will not be for several days that the boy will return to bear away his letter.

CENOTAPH. The town buries its dead in the churchyard, or in small family plots. On Sunday mornings the faithful leaving church often place flowers or other tokens on the graves of loved ones. In summer, the sexton cuts the grass in the churchyard, out of respect to the departed and so that mourners may have access to the graves. During the blue afternoons of winter, the pastor may look up from the desk where he reads and prepares his sermons, seeing through his window a bare tree and headstones; then he will rise to draw the curtains and stoke the fire. At funerals, the pastor wonders at each mute coffin lowered into the earth even as he reads from the Bible, his voice louder than the soft weeping of widows and orphans. Yet in the churchyard are several markers over solid ground where nothing lies but tree roots, rocks, and worms. It is to one of these, a simple granite stone erected only three years ago, that the boy sometimes comes, tracing a finger over the name chiseled there.

DAYS. Merchant ships along the channel, hard bread, the light at the top of the tower, the morning's catch of fish in a cart, navigational maps and depth-soundings, chimney smoke rising from bare trees, a cap and woolen muffler, the endless sound of wind: days pass.

OTHER COUNTRIES. Nights, now, the boy may find himself lost in the dunes, or wandering the streets of the shipping port, where sailors enter smoky taverns along the harbor and oil lamps burn in many windows. From the darkness comes the murmur of voices, or the calls of the longshoremen. The boy strolls the piers, where even at late hours men unload goods from the holds of ships. A ship may arrive at any time, bearing men who have seen distant cities and weeks of empty seas. The boy looks for traces of other countries in the eyes of men who pass him, or in their dress or manner, but he cannot read these faces. He imagines the sway of a ship on the waves, himself somewhere inside it, sleeping under skies where the stars are different, aligned in ways he cannot guess.

TERMINATION. As he sorts among the coins on the table for the boy's customary wage, the lighthouse keeper does not know—hoping as he does that the letter he has just handed to the boy will reach its desired end—that the arrangement the two have will not last the week.

OVERHEAD. The sky along the coast stretches away over the ocean for miles, and clouds blow in from all directions or else linger over the land for days. On the beach, a person may sit on an old blanket, idly watching clouds stretch and tear, or, if the day is windy, scud toward the horizon. On summer afternoons, the appearance of thick clouds over the ocean, their undersides dark, signifies thunderstorms. Mares' tails also portend rainy weather, days when the fishermen do not venture into deep waters. Many of the town's fishermen believe that clouds breaking up in the first light of morning indicate that a full day's catch of fish will be taken in the forenoon. But the tourist on the blanket does not consider omens in weather. To him the clouds assume the shapes of animals, or objects, one cloud before his eyes turning from a flower into a fishtail, and then, while his eyes cast to another cloud in the form of a house, the first cloud has become something else entirely. The lighthouse keeper, standing in the lantern gallery, may watch the same clouds, though in them he sees a sailing ship, or a tree, or else notices only their color, the gray blending into white.

BOXES. Into crates and boxes goes the library of books, and later the lighthouse keeper finds that some of the nails used to seal the lids of the crates have scratched the bindings, and in one case penetrated the leaves. The blackbird, its cage draped with heavy muslin, is placed by the door to the lighthouse, while the lighthouse keeper removes other personal effects from the four rooms of the tower. The young men from town he has hired to bear away his goods lift the boxes into the back of the wagon, then stand patting the horse's nose. Here on the end of land the wind pulls tears from their eyes, and they are eager to return to town. But the lighthouse keeper lingers in the lantern gallery, his hand clutching the rail while below him waves break on the shore with no sound.

GHOST STORIES. In the tavern, a man speaking softly tells how the night before the wreck of the *Coral*, one member of the crew dreamed of nine coffins floating on the waves; he knew that one of the coffins was his own, for on top of it rested his favorite pipe. In the morning, the man related his dream to his wife before sailing on the *Coral* that noon. At the pier his wife begged him to stay, but the man was bound by his contract with the ship owner. When the *Coral* foundered in high seas just beyond the channel at dusk, all hands were lost. News came to town in the form of bits of wreckage washed ashore. Only nine bodies were recovered—one of which was that of the sailor who had dreamed of nine coffins. The *Coral* may sometimes be sighted on stormy nights, sailing from the channel into the open seas, manned by shadowy forms dripping seawater. They do not speak, but their eyes warn sailors away before the entire vision fades. The speaker's voice trails off, and he drinks to wet his tongue. The men gathered in the tavern are quiet for a moment, staring into their mugs of beer, before another begins the tale of one of the first keepers at the lighthouse, cut off from town by a severe winter many years ago, who was found with his throat slit—by his own hand—when the light went out and men from town forced their way through snowdrifts higher than a man's head to reach the tower. Now, the speaker claims, the lighthouse keeper will wake to find the works polished, when he had planned to do that very task himself. Or, at night, the keeper will hear footsteps endlessly pacing the lantern gallery, though should he dare to investigate he will discover nothing.

THE LIGHTHOUSE KEEPER. The new lighthouse keeper, the townspeople think, keeps a splendid light. In his uniform he can be seen days walking the grounds of the lighthouse or rowing his skiff into the channel to check on the buoys; his mustache is fine and his voice, as he waves and calls out to passersby, clear. To anyone who asks—especially the young women spending the summer by the shore—he will show the brass works in the lantern gallery, wiping with a cloth smudges or stains invisible to the eyes of his guests. The townspeople do not often recall that until recently another man kept the light at the point of the channel; they did not often see and so did not remark much upon the former keeper, save to wonder at such a man as would be content to stay in a drafty tower all winter, with no visitor but an errand-boy. Their memories are short, except concerning the locations of the best cod banks, or the number of years that have passed since the worst blizzard struck the coast, and even among these facts there is seldom agreement.

UNEMPLOYMENT. The position which the boy held with the former lighthouse keeper does not interest the new keeper when the boy, seeking further employment, calls at the tower. The lighthouse keeper, annoyed at this distraction, tells the boy to be off and then turns his back to finish hoisting the weather pennants, which signify clear skies. Behind him, the lighthouse keeper can still feel the boy's presence. Whistling to himself, he pretends not to notice, and lashes the end of the rope to the pole. He stands facing the sea for a moment, listening to the surf below him and twisting the end of his mustache, and when he turns again he sees that the boy has walked some distance away without his hearing. The lighthouse keeper gives the matter no more thought, and does not see the boy again, though the boy often returns to the lighthouse at night, watching the silhouette of the lighthouse keeper in the lantern gallery.

ALMS. The boy's mother has not stirred from her bed for some days, though the pastor does not know this when he brings a fish stew prepared by one of his own servants. She does not rise when the pastor knocks, and he opens the door slowly, removing his hat and peering into the gloom: behind a curtain he sees a woman lying in bed as if asleep or ill. He sets the stew pot on the dusty table, recalling as he does so that this woman is the one whose husband was lost several years past, and whom some in town claim is mad with grief. He remembers also a boy, young and quiet at the time of his father's death, a small shadow among the few mourners that day the pastor performed the last rites, but certainly of working age now. To poverty the pastor is accustomed, for nearly all of his parishioners are the town's fishermen and their families, and it is only in the summer months that the wealthy tourists attend services. Yet the dona- tions received by the church from these affluent summer families allow the pastor to administer aid to the needy of his parish during the hard winters. Now, observing the shabby state of the house, and realizing that the woman's son must work from sunup to sunset to support his ailing mother, the pastor decides to use church funds to hire help for the woman—a cleaning-girl, or a nurse, perhaps. He steps closer to wake the woman from her fitful sleep and to open a window to admit some healthy air; dust and the stale reek of unwashed bedding fill the room. The boy's mother opens her eyes as he draws near, and starts up in her bed, believing for a moment that the shade she sees before her is her husband restored to her: then she screams at the pastor's outstretched hand.

THE STRANGER. Occasionally, the idle men in town and the retired fishermen loitering in the square notice an unfamiliar man, who carries one arm curled always toward his chest, entering the general store, where he receives small parcels from the clerk at the counter. The man usually enters the post office next, and is then seen walking across the square again, packages and mail carried awkwardly in the crook of his good arm. The man does not speak to those who observe him; indeed, he does not even lift his head, and most likely does not notice those who follow him with their gaze, so intent does he seem on bearing away what he carries, though no one knows what the brown wrappers conceal, nor where the man carries them. This man is unfamiliar to the men from town but he does not seem unlike them, as do certain men who arrive from the shipping port for one reason or another, stepping into the dusty square from a carriage, or riding up on a fine horse. Yet this fact only makes him more mysterious to those who watch him, as if an outsider had lived amongst them for many years, learning their customs and habits without their knowledge or consent, finally appearing in their midst as one of their own.

AFIELD. The waves refuse to yield the voice of his father and so the boy shouts into the din of breakers on rocks. For days now he has wandered farther and farther afield, roaming the lands from the shipping port to the lighthouse, sleeping in barns and boathouses, roasting crabs and gulls' eggs over driftwood fires on the beach. Once he looked in the window of his own house at night, where a woman he did not know stood over the stove while his mother sat in a chair, wrapped in blankets. Steam fogged the glass until the two figures became only blurred shapes, one standing and one seated, and for a moment the boy believed he had been sleeping and was just now waking, as though he had suffered another of the visions haunting his mind. Then the wind had chilled him, and he left town for the thickets, where wind cannot penetrate the tangled growth. In the days since, he has followed trails that he has never before noticed, meandering paths through the dunes, the sand unmarked by any feet but his own. One night, as gathering clouds hasten the arrival of darkness, the boy follows the trail into a hollow, where a small house has been abandoned, sand in a deep drift before the door. The boy climbs through a gaping window, the glass broken long ago, and, wrapping his coat about him, curls to sleep on the warped boards of the floor.

FOG. Along this part of the coast, many days are dim until afternoon, when the heat of the sun burns off the mists, or else a fog may blow in and transform a clear day. The fog muffles and distorts sounds, and a man walking along the road to the shipping port may hear footsteps he thinks follow him, yet which are the steps of another man whose shadow will soon appear before him. On the sea, sailors may hear buoys ringing, but cannot pinpoint the direction from which the bell sounds. In thick banks of fog, moisture drips from trees and dampens coats and trousers, and some say the vapors are unhealthy to breathe. The superstitious believe that fog conceals from sight many evil things best left unseen, and do not walk abroad until the sun is bright again. Yet the children in town often play in the gloom, chasing each other blindly, running toward the shape of a bush which they believe is a crouching child. The children have their own superstitions, and wait for the fog to lift, for it is at this moment when sunlight and shadow mix that they believe things hidden are sometimes forgotten by the vanishing mists, and become visible to ordinary sight—though they also believe that one of them may be lost at such a juncture, and disappear, a voice forever calling on other foggy days, but never discovered.

THE NURSE AND THE MOTHER. Out of her mind, the nurse thinks, out of her mind. She sits daily by the sick woman's bed, wiping the woman's brow with a damp cloth to keep down the fever which has seized her. In bed, the woman lies still for hours, eyelids barely fluttering and her breast nearly still; then she may rise, thrashing against sheets tucked in tightly by the nurse, wrapping her arms in knots of fabric. One morning the nurse may struggle to run a brush through the woman's matted hair, while the next the woman may not move as the nurse bathes her, or feeds her spoonfuls of broth. Most afternoons the pastor comes by to check on the woman, who at times raves about the sea which she says has claimed all she loved. The doctor has come twice from the shipping port and diagnosed fever and hysteria, telling the nurse and the pastor to soothe the woman's nerves. Stimulation of any sort must be kept to a minimum, he says, drawing the curtains shut. The pastor has made inquiries about the town, asking neighbors and parishioners about relatives, though no one knows the names of the woman's people, or where they may live. Some mention a young boy; others say that the woman's son left for a job in the shipping port or in Providence, or is on the crew of a ship sailing to the West Indies. The pastor nods and wonders what can be done. Soon he will come by the small house less often, his mind on other matters relating to his church. The nurse he has hired to tend to the woman is capable and industrious, and the doctor has advised him that the woman needs rest. And so the days the nurse has stayed in the house stretch into weeks, and months. To her it seems that she has always looked after this woman, confined to her bed where she sometimes weeps at the sound of waves, clenching her hands into fists hidden beneath the blankets. At these times the nurse takes from the night-stand a book, and, opening to a certain page, clears her throat and begins to read.

THE HERMIT. The townspeople do not remember a time before the hermit roamed the dunes south of town, frightening occasional travelers and searching the beaches for items washed ashore. Fishermen in the tavern tell of smoke rising from the trees in a place of no dwellings, or of sheep stolen in the night. Summer visitors sometimes claim to have observed a strange figure, clothed in rags, while they were collecting seashells or smooth pebbles on the beach. Mothers bathing reluctant children speak in whispers about the hermit, whom they say will come in the night for the small boys and girls he sells to the merchant ships, or to the Indians, or whom he eats in the shack he inhabits somewhere in the dunes, which no one has ever found. The tale grows and changes with each telling until the mother, scrubbing her child's elbows and knees with a sponge, is no longer certain whether such a person exists or ever existed; yet her child does not move, intent as he is on her every word. The pastor wonders if the hermit is a religious fanatic, though he thinks it more likely that the hermit is simply a debtor, an eccentric, or perhaps an escaped convict. At times he is tempted to follow the trails which are said to crisscross the dunes, but he does not know what he would say to this hermit should he find him.

VERSIONS OF THE SAME STORY. In the tavern, the bartender listens year after year to stories which sound similar to one another, or which suggest to his mind other conversations he has overheard, or which stir in his memory a specific place or moment of time. He wipes cloths across rings of water on wood, collects empty beer mugs while some voice continues its tale, the listeners still and silent if the story is told well, impatient if it is not. Perhaps it is when the lighthouse keeper—his mustache now a bit untidy, his uniform worn with use—joins the fishermen and the drunks at the tavern one night, complaining that he has been dismissed from his position for supporting the wrong party in the recent elections, that memories recall another keeper at the light, a one-handed man known by none in town but the boy who delivered his mail. About this man many stories are told, voices rising to drown the others out. One fisherman recounts seeing this former keeper on the road to the shipping port one afternoon. The keeper mentioned, while the two men shared a flask of whisky, that he was headed north to his own people, where he had once been the son of a potato farmer. Potato farmer! another man interrupts, explaining that the keeper's hand was cut off for thievery during his sailing days, that he had once been on a ship with the keeper sometime after the loss of the hand, and that the story of his mutilation entertained many of the crew during long watches. The keeper was nothing more than a rascal with friends in high places, the speaker says, a man who knew how to bend the system to his own advantage: otherwise, how could such a man attain an important post? A man at the edge of the circle begins to speak, his voice at first too quiet to be heard by many, though soon everyone has stopped talking to listen to his tale of a sailor, drunk on brandy, who murdered another man with a barrel stave on a Manhattan wharf, and who, fleeing the authorities, came here, where he disguised himself as a simple lighthouse keeper. Here another man sets down his mug and says that he knows this former keeper, and that the man lives in town now, in a small cottage not far from the tavern, where he keeps a blackbird which can recite the letters of the alphabet, and which knows words no man has spoken. Several voices demand to know why they have not seen a one-handed man about, nor a speaking bird, and are not satisfied by the speaker's explanation that the keeper is a quiet sort who rarely leaves his home. A few men stand and put on their coats; other men call for more beer. The bartender removes the emptied mugs and fills new ones from the tap. When he has served the men he steps back from the circle of faces and voices to listen doubtfully to the next story they have already begun to tell.

READING. The pleasure of the act of reading does not leave the lighthouse keeper, if many other pleasures may have left him. Often he looks up from his book surprised to find that the sun is rising and he has not yet slept.

He passes hours searching through books for a familiar phrase, a recognizable character, a remembered tone—yet in each new book he reads, many phrases sound familiar, certain characters remind him of those he recalls from other stories, and one author's tone may echo any other's. Though he still desires more than anything to find the one story he remembers from his childhood, he is no longer certain if such a story exists. He has read so much that he is not sure if what he remembers is a real story, or one he dreamed, or one he invented in his own mind while his mother read an entirely different story.

THE LIGHTHOUSE. The lighthouse at the end of the peninsula has stood, in one form or another, for many years. When the structure has been destroyed or ruined by poor construction and planning, or been endangered by the erosion of the coastline, it has been repaired or rebuilt. Yet the location is always essentially the same: the point of land commanding a view of both the sea and the channel ships must navigate to reach the shipping port. To the townspeople, some of whom may have assisted those contracted to repair or rebuild the structure, the lighthouse is the same lighthouse that has stood since before the days of the Revolution, performing the same function. Few of the townspeople have been inside the lighthouse, where traces remain of the keepers who have for a time lived there. These keepers come and go, appointed by one or another politician, or dying and passing the position to a widow or son. In a dusty corner of the lighthouse may lie a scrap of a logbook entry written during a storm fifty years past, or a ring slipped from the finger of another keeper, or a single black feather. Anyone entering the lighthouse will feel at once the sense of past times: the iron hinges turned to rust, the hollowed stone steps. The echoes of many different feet blur into one echo along the stairs to the lantern gallery, where, year after year, the light circles.

# DUNDEE

It was the first time she ever tasted honey, in that house, from a jar her uncle had collected himself, the end of his finger dipped into the jar and brought to her mouth. And then it was bread and honey, honey spooned on oatmeal, honey stirred into tea. She was seven years old. Her uncle's house had no bathroom but a trail through blackberry bushes downhill to the outhouse. Her uncle would walk in only one room upstairs, where in places the crossbeams showed through holes in the floor. She wrapped her hand around his fingers and tapped a toe against a board gone soft and powdery. Sun shone through chinks in the walls, where clapboards had fallen or been pulled slowly loose by climbing bittersweet. Mice nested behind the plaster; at night she heard them scratching.

One of her uncle's kittens would come and crouch in the doorway, its eyes glowing green in the light of the moon. From other walls hung strips of pink insulation the kittens liked to claw. Her uncle hammered, tenpenny nails between his teeth. Wires dangled. She drew splinters from the floor into her bare feet, her uncle holding a pin in the flame of a match to dig in her skin to where his tweezers could reach. At night he lit candles and read her stories.

To begin: Once upon a time a girl visited her uncle in a falling-down house. Her uncle did not own the house but, on the first day of every month, paid another man for its use. The front stairs were warped and rotted, boards were missing from the porch, shingles had slipped from the roof. Squirrels nested in the chimney and a skunk lived in the cellar. Grass and weeds grew tall against the windows. Maple branches knocked the eaves in a wind. Her uncle patched the crumbling foundation with cement he mixed in a plastic bucket while she poured the water. But mostly what the girl remembered about the house, years later, were the bugs: crickets and grasshoppers, mosquitoes humming in her ears at night, the horsefly that bit her neck, Junebugs blundering into lamps, moths in the closets, spiders in the corners, tent caterpillars in the birch trees, dead houseflies stuck to loops of flypaper hanging from the kitchen ceiling, cicadas whose shells she found clinging to the spruce, bumblebees that reminded her always of the taste of honey.

She asked me not to write this story, and then she asked me to write a story about her, a story for her. "To tell it would ruin it," she said, and then, while we lay together in the dark that first year, our legs a tangle beneath the blankets, she told me the story of the girl who went to stay summer nights at the house in the woods—the house where she could lie on the dusty floor upstairs and watch the moon watching her through the window where no glass was, the house where one night a raccoon carried off one of her uncle's kittens while, barefoot, he chased after it into the dark, the house where in the morning she would wake in her twisted-up sleeping bag to find the house empty, her uncle already outside, weeding the garden on his hands and knees. "But there was no garden," she said. "You're forgetting."

In that house, she let burrs and pine pitch catch in her hair so that later her mother would have to cut it short, like her uncle's, she said. As the branches against our window began to stand out against the just-bluing sky, as her voice faded into sleep after hours of talking, she told me how her uncle woke her in the dark one morning to watch the moment the sun bled over the hills. And how one afternoon, to see what would happen, she and her uncle tore pieces of stale bread and scattered them along the pine-needled path into the woods as they walked, though when they returned all of the scraps were untouched.

Her uncle told her a story: That summer, while he drove his pickup truck down the dirt road that led to his house, a butterfly veered into his path. He stopped his truck and watched the butterfly for a moment, and then it flew down the road away from him. He told her how he stepped lightly on the gas pedal to follow those hinged wings before they vanished into the leafy shadows. He pushed the speedometer up to thirty, then thirty-five miles an hour, and still the butterfly led him up the hill, a tiny orange blur weaving under arched branches. When he came near his house he watched as the butterfly lifted over his roof and disappeared.

But she did not tell me which stories to tell, or which stories to keep secret. She told me to write about the pretty brown-eyed girl, and so I am. But she did not tell me what those brown eyes saw at the house in the woods, the summer she was seven.

The road was closed from the first day of November, when men came and locked a gate across it, to the last day of April. The road climbed into the foothills of the mountains, and even the foothills were covered with snow through the long winters. Then her uncle would have to leave, not only because snow would blow through his windows and across his crooked floors, but because he could no longer get to town. He didn't know where he would go once the leaves began to fall. He didn't pay the man who owned the house much money, and he didn't mind the way rain leaked through the roof or the way he had to brace one sagging wall with wood beams. Her uncle was poor and he knew that the houses in the valley, near town, cost more to rent than he could afford, and so he didn't like to think of the coming cold, the storms that would leave ice coating bare branches or snow in huge drifts on the road. But this is not a winter's tale, with frost glazing the windows, dead leaves and gray skies, both of us putting our feet on the hot bricks of the hearth and drawing our chairs closer together—not a story where every word spoken turns to white clouds that float away on the wind, not a story of those months when the sun traces only a brief arc across the sky and does not light anything.

On the walls inside the house her uncle had hung a seed calendar and the pictures she had spent rainy afternoons drawing for him. A deer, a kitten, a face at the window of a house surrounded by trees. But one window, they decided, was itself a painting—the green fields they could see far below them, one silver-topped silo, the dark trees, the mountains rising behind everything, the sky. At sunset they pulled chairs to the window and leaned their feet against the wall.

"Just make it any house," she told me, "any old house in the woods."

In August she walked down the road with her uncle, picking blueberries and dropping them into one of her uncle's hats. Her uncle told her about the bears that took their cubs to eat blueberries in the woods. He showed her how to whistle with her thumbs and a blade of grass. Shimmy up a skinny birch, he said, and when she reached the top it would bend down to bring her back to the ground. She kicked rocks; small clouds of dust rose. Some of the blueberries she ate straight from the bush. He saw a maple with a few red leaves and pointed to it. When they had walked back to the falling-down house, he took the blueberries from his hat and washed them; they filled two bowls. He poured cream over them and spooned a bit of sugar into each bowl. She watched the crystals turn gray and melt into the cream. "But there were no blueberries," she said. "That's your story, not mine."

And each night, by the time her uncle had spoken the last word in the story and shut the cover of the book, she was already asleep—the faded blanket pulled to her chin covered by wavering candlelight and shadows. Years later, while we lay in bed each night, a stretched rectangle of moonlight falling across our bodies, I looked at the blank ceiling and told the same few stories I knew—again and again, believing she still wanted to hear them—until I heard her slow breathing over the shoulder she'd raised between us.

One of the last nights of summer her uncle woke her in the dark and brought her outside to watch the meteor showers. It was cold for August, even there in the foot-hills of the mountains, and they wrapped themselves in wool blankets. The grass was wet with dew, and seeds stuck to the soaked cuffs of her jeans. Her uncle lay on his back, and she rested her head on his belly. Trees, and the skewed angle of the roof, were dark shadows against dark sky, rising from the edges of her vision toward the blurs of stars. Her uncle pointed. And then they both waited for the sky to fall, for a piece of rock and ice to burn itself up in a bright spark as the Earth pulled it toward them.

Once upon a time, I told her, a young woman and a young man lived together. They had little money and their apartment was small, two rooms only: from the bathtub they could touch the bed, the man's head brushed the ceilings, and at the kitchen table there was room for only one chair. Sometimes one of them watched the other eat, and then they switched places, but most often they ate alone. The radiator in the bedroom didn't work, and they wore sweaters and wool hats to bed in January. At all hours, the man and the woman who lived in the next apartment fought, and the sounds of these arguments seeped through the walls while they tried to sleep, or read books, or speak in quiet voices. "But didn't that ruin it?" she asked. "Almost," I told her, because soon the young woman and the young man began to argue themselves, and the low ceiling and close walls, the branches scraping the glass of their windows, and the nights when their breath clouded the air made them forget everything but their unhappiness. But then they decided to move away, to another town, a town where they would have room for two chairs in wide, quiet rooms. Their new apartment was bigger, and in the afternoons sunlight fell through their windows, but after only a week they began to hear the fighting of the couple who lived upstairs; the woman who lived downstairs would sometimes cry and cry for hours, or play the piano for hours, and all these sounds drifted into their apartment through the heating vents, rolling along their wooden floors like the ropes of dust that they soon stopped sweeping. The young woman began to sleep on the couch, where she said it was more peaceful. At night the young man would read books into the early morning, and sometimes when he turned off his lamp he was surprised to see light at the crack under his door: he hadn't known she was still awake. "That's a sad story," she said, "but I'm sure there was more to it than that."

Years after her uncle had moved out of that house, when she had a truck of her own, she drove up the dirt road. The road had just been opened for the season, but in places it was still washed out, so she drove slowly, the way her uncle had, and rolled down her window. Buds were just forming on the trees, and the woods were tinged with green. She parked her truck on the grass where her uncle had parked his truck those summer days, and walked around the house, looking in the broken windows. The bittersweet's woody stalks now covered the clapboards and waved new shoots from the edge of the roof. Her uncle's supports still shored the sagging wall. So much paint had peeled that parts of the walls were bare, but when she leaned her hand against the house, flecks of red stuck to her skin. The woods seemed closer, as if waiting for the day a strong wind would blow the house down, when the ragweed and blackberries and sugar maple seedlings would grow over the collapsed timbers and crumbled fieldstone. When she walked back to the front of the house she saw another truck parked next to hers. A man opened the door and stepped out. "What are you doing here?" he yelled. "This is private property!" She looked at him for a moment and didn't speak, then got into her truck and drove away. In her mirror she watched the man watching her, his hands on his hips, until she rounded a bend in the road. "But didn't that ruin it?" I asked. "No," she said. "It's still there." And then—a few years after the man who owned the house, the man her uncle had paid each month, had yelled at her—on another spring day, she told me this story while we drove along the road to the falling-down house in the woods.

❄

But now even more years have passed and it is another summer, a summer of days so humid the hills fade into gray shapes and dew lingers for hours on the leaves. It is a summer not of stories told aloud but of stories read alone in silence under a tree's shifting shade, or at night, in bed, while moths circle the lamp. A summer when she has gone; when I stay in this room writing stories for someone who will not read them. I try to think of what I could have said—of everything left out of stories. Can I include the photograph she once took of that house, the photograph she gave to me to recall an April day, to halt that slow ruin? She never told me what happened to her uncle, as that summer turned to fall, and, though I met him the same day I saw that house, I did not think to ask. The sun burns through the haze and falls across my hand, here, on the page. A spider climbs the screen and outside a catbird screeches from a fencepost. Beyond my window trees in full leaf stir in a faint wind. I try to imagine what that house must look like now, several years after I first saw it—its roof collapsed, only one bare timber still reaching up; sumac and bittersweet covering what remains of the walls; the fieldstone chimney fallen into a pile of rubble; the grass taller than my waist. And, though I cannot believe it now, I tell myself that all stories must end.

# THE FISHERMAN
# AND HIS WIFE

PROSPERO. Now I arise:
Sit still, and hear the last of our sea-sorrow.
—Shakespeare, *The Tempest*

Bayberry has bent, bowed, for years to the shapes this
wind blows, and rises only to my knees above lichen-
spattered granite. Sumac, juniper, beach plum—here,
these patches of thatchy growth; here, the stray strands
of marram, seed-strewn from shore beaches to find the
sandy crevices on this island and so gift me with a bit of
bleached greenery. East, in a blurred line, the sea reaches
the sky at last. Far to the west, waves whiten the base of
bare bluffs. Between this coastline and the distant swells
stand only a cluster of dwarf pine and the four walls I
raised, the steep-peaked roof edged with rusty tin. Smoke
rises and is dispersed. This wind catches everything in
it—smoke, gulls and terns and petrels that can only fly

with it, words from a man's mouth. Loose, a wind-worried pebble will carve a channel through rock.

The briny soak of storm that woke me this dawn has become a slap and suck of surf on rock, a hedge of dark clouds the wind has swept past. But hours ago, as it dragged its rains over my roof and ran in runnels down my windowpanes, I pulled on my boots and, slicker dull in early light, circled the broken beach and scouted secret pools to see what the waters would bring me. Now, as they have ebbed, my island, at its southwest corner, has reclaimed another acre lapped by the sea.

This wood—caught, here, in the tide line's drag of litter—may have floated years, crossed oceans, the cast-off post of an Irish farmer's fence. Or risen from weedy deeps, a plank from a sunken schooner, the nail that held it in place finally rusted through. The bark-stripped limb of some tree, fallen into a sea-bound river. And storm-struck waves washed it—barnacled, foam-flecked, salt-stained, polished—to land, this morning; to my feet.

I heft the wood to my shoulder; head back to my shingled cabin, where later I will pull my three-legged stool near the stove and lay my knife upon my knee; where now I sling the wood into the scrap bin in the kitchen's corner. The stunted pine are the island's only trees, and these I do not cut.

My wife did not want to come here, and, when she did come, came only once she'd assured that those things she feared she must leave would come with her. In soil I spaded, one summer morning, from her mother's inland garden, then drove to the coast to heap into my dinghy—in this soil, rowed the mile to the island, then circled with stones and mortar to protect it from the wear of winds and waves, she planted the pine seedlings she'd burlap-wrapped and smuggled from her mother's home. By the door, she pressed into more of this soft earth the charcoal seeds of morning glories, and, as the vines grew, trained them to twine around themselves, to climb and cling to a lattice she leaned against the wall, green leaves rippling in a breeze.

She stitched curtains to hang before the glass I'd salvaged for the sashes, pieced quilts from scraps of my old dungarees and the oddments of calico and gingham she'd stashed in the trunks she brought. On the wall she tacked a square-folded map, those brown hilltops and green woods she'd surrendered: this map's only blue the meandering threads of streams, the small beads of ponds. In the letters they sent, her sisters would fold a pressed maple leaf, veiny and red; tuck an acorn cap for whistling, a tiny hemlock cone. Soon, our mantel, our sills, were trimmed with the forest's leavings, gathered by careful hands and dispatched to her here. When—salt-rimed and rope-burnt, fishy, iridescent with scales—I returned each night, the cabin smelled not of sea airs but of her homely food warming on the woodstove.

Winter, the spray froze to the shingles of our cabin, glazed glass panes with frost to turn the slight sunlight blue; slashes of icy weather and the channel's churning waters kept us bound by ceilings and walls, a stretch of planked floor, oil lamps' dusky smoke, the cans a cupboard could contain. My wife pined for land, the silence of a snowed field, dark hills faint-formed at dusk, the feel of earth instead of this sea-dashed rock, saltwater-sticky, wave-slicked, raw with fogs. She wanted the hush-tap of tree branches at night beyond her windows, not the unending tales of winds nor the ceaseless seas' seethe. But I did not guess those words she spoke as the year turned and the smoke-smell of burning hardwood clung to the wool we wore: "No child I bear will grow up webbed and gilled." It was her father came to fetch her, a rare February morning of mackerel skies, faint sun and low tides, the edges of the island black with abandoned muck. Her father did not step from the skiff, but the boy from the nearest coastal village who'd guided him here knocked on the door where the suitcase she'd had packed a week already stood.

I stoke the stove and fill the kettle. The radio is hiss and whine, low pops, a voice—at times I wonder who it is has landed on the island and speaks to me, but this talk is always of the weather: approaching rains and cold spells, five-foot whitecaps, daily means, falling barometers. For news I wait for Bill Quincy, who every two weeks arrives in his boat, bringing whatever mail has collected in my box, vegetables in summer and cordwood in fall, books his wife has thumbed, foil-sealed chocolate and tins of tea, oil for my tools, spools of heavy thread, turpentine, boot wax and boxes of waterproofed matches, pies the villages' widows have baked, sheets of sandpaper from fine to coarse. Seven years now my dinghy has stayed dry, overturned, roped and wrapped in canvas, in my shed next to stacks of split wood.

Bill Quincy takes my carvings to the tourist shacks on the coastal highways, to the antique galleries in the villages where, he tells me, the proprietors arrange them in display windows next to lobster traps and patches of netting, scrimshaw, salt-etched buoys and brass sextants. He brings his ledger book, the columns of blotchy ink

where in his scraggy hand he has recorded the amounts
of his purchases for me and the prices my carvings have
claimed. A balance in my favor he pays out from his
wallet in wrinkled bills. On debts he is easy.

"Not carvings," he says. "Neither art," I tell him. For
it is simply that my fingers close upon whichever length
of storm-drifted lumber heaped in my woodbin my eye
first fixes, and my knife's stone-scraped blade trims curls
of pinholed wood to shape the fanned feathers of a gull's
wing or a gannet's smooth bill, a kittiwake or shearwater
in flight. Some, wings spread for balance, I dangle from
the rafters on looped and knotted twine; they turn slow
circles. I pour Bill Quincy a mug of tea, sweep shavings
and sawdust into a box to cradle the packed birds.

"Always birds?" Bill Quincy once asked.

"Birds or you," I told him. "You're my guests."

No child has come to see this mussel-pooled rib of
rock, these meager and unnamed acres, and so I think I
never had a child, never a daughter to stretch and weave
seaweed into mats, to search shells for pearls, to hear
among the waves the voices of the drowned; never a son
to bait a bent pin and tug crabs from heaving seas, to
dive for shipwrecked doubloons. Any child imagined in
a sea-rimmed bed would want to visit those waters that
had harbored the smaller waters in which the still-blind
child first swam; and so I think I am no father. For this
rock is no breeding ground for anything but the herring
gulls which return each year, their speckled eggs in grass-
lined sand scrapes or cradled in stony ledges.

That first fall I wrote a letter to my wife, closing it
in wax paper to keep it from damp; I rowed it to shore,
posted it to that address where pines shade mossy lawns:

in late October, her morning glories still flowered, pale blue trumpets nodding from leafy doorposts and lintel. Every week, until December's storm-angry swells kept me home, I looked for her response in the village's whitewashed office. None came.

Wood, wood, wood, wood. I can whittle a block, a branch—knife, knife, chisel and file—and, at a skewed wing or a splintered beak, pitch it into the stove to warm my spread hands. Or, on a day of Indian summer, cut and sculpt a stick of firewood if my scrap bin is empty.

Joist and beam, post and girt, lath, stud and rafter, clapboard and shingle—so did I build this cabin, raw wood to shift and creak like the trees of the forests my wife had quit.

"Once," I sometimes remind Bill Quincy, when he's steered his boat to my pier, bringing a tin of Prince Albert for my pipe, "the King of England forbade settlers on these shores from felling their tallest trees." It is a tale any old-timer could recite, but still Bill Quincy will listen to me tell it. Any white pine two or more feet thick his surveyors marked for the masts of His Majesty's navy; they cleared woods for fields, stacked the holds of cargo vessels with hundred-foot pines for shipyards across the sea. But, though that old-growth pine has been long logged, the pastures are woodlands once more: I can recall the woo of my not-yet-wife, the two of us seated on hand-set stone walls, years old, beneath a lace of leafy branches where nothing grew but ferns and laurel. Sea-born myself, whelped of curling breakers and wind-scoured dunes, I had traced a river's meander upstream to search for a woman where the water fell, funneling between rocks into a pool edged with orange needles.

"And that's where I found her," I have told Bill Quincy.

Then, I pressed to her ear the shell of a whelk I had carried, to charm her with the spell of the ocean it held.

Those dawns I rose from the boat of our bed, one bare foot on the frosty floor and then the other, my wife would roll in her sleep; toss, tangled in the snarl of blankets, as her near-closed eyes sought me out in the tin-blue of morning. "Don't go," she would say. "Listen to that wind today. Can't you hear those breakers?" But already I was breathing a fire into the belly of the stove: kindling catching, papers blackly dwindling to nothing; I was tugging a shirt over that I had slept in, buttoning pants, stamping feet into boots; I was steeping tea, picking its leaves from my tongue—I was slipped into my slicker, I was all wool and rubber, fastened and zipped; and then, the door bolt-latched behind me, gone. It was only in the evening's dark, as, adrift in our blankets, we floated ourselves once again on the mattress, that my wife said, "And if you drown one day, how will I pilot the boat to land by myself?"

Evening, even inside, the wind has discovered the waxed wicks of my candles: one skips and flutters; another, snuffed, smokes. Kerosene burns in a chimney of sooty glass. Beyond these wavering lights, past the jars on my windowsill, I can see only the pinpricks of shore homes' electric lamps, the twelve-mile lighthouse's circling beam, a planed-away pinch of moon. For the business of only one customer, the power company claims, they cannot stretch undersea cable.

My wife had been gone a year when I stopped putting out to sea each morning, swimming my wave-doused boat to those offshore banks where, beneath a squall of gulls, men drew nets heavy with cod and haddock over their gunwales, spilling silver-white fish onto their decks. I tired of those round eyes, blind to the sight of our clouds; of flared gills, rippling fins; of that writhe and struggle—the muscled bend of fish into my boots, tail-slaps against wood, the thunk and thunk of them around me, the blood we hosed off the deck each afternoon. None ever spoke to me; none kept a coin in its mouth; none would grant a wish for its release—none brought me anything but stink and a scant weekly wage.

Those months my wife was first missing, I fed her knee-high pines wellwater from the dented can she had used—believing, then, that their healthy boughs would move her to stay, when she returned with our child and saw them. It was not until years later—one afternoon, as I spilled a waste of fresh water over that strange inland earth—that I noticed the pines' needled fingers. Tipped the pale green of new growth, they pointed to the circles the gulls inscribed upon the sky. Below the water-pocked soil, their roots had grasped rock; what had seemed a worthless dowry was, I now saw, a prize. So too, I had always burned any shore-spun wood that reached me for warmth; now it seemed a message from my wife, the timber of her homeland drifted to me bit by bit, each scrap another letter in a language I am still learning. Wait, the messages said. Not yet. Turning the wood in my hands, I read its surfaces, then carved it into shapes to fly back to her—never dreaming that my hair would whiten while I waited for a word from her; that

her seedlings would better me in height. I still waste
water on the pines.

Again, this morning, a cloudwash of rain melts into
green seas. Bundled in the sweater Bill Quincy's wife
knit me in exchange for a tern with a laughing beak,
I gaze through streaked glass at the close horizon and
imagine a house in a thick wood, the sway of tousled
pines, the sound of the drops through fall's ragged leaves,
a child grown and gone from the rooms where a mother
sits by a window, looking out at the rain. But this child,
the salt beat of its blood, the gray cast to the eyes the only
gifts I gave it—this child was no child, no wake of my
wave. Some days I think I may as well carve the shape
of a boy or a girl from the trees she planted as wait for a
child to wash up on these remote shores.

But what I have told is only part of the story. For what man
wants to admit he was wrong, and who wants to hear his
confession? Listen now. Once I stopped fishing, I exiled
myself to this Elba, this St. Helena. Hours unfolded; the
sea, retreating and arriving, was the only voice I heard.
Disowned by my wife, I married the waves unrolling
themselves against my shores, married the winter blows
that rattled my windows and kept me close to the stove,
married the mists. I married the nighttime whispers of
the radio; turning their pages again and again, I married
the few books on my shelf. I married myself. I watched
passing boats, liners and freighters hazy with distance,
each voyage near or not; imagined the press of people on
a pier as a ship approached. But each day that I waited, I
never thought that someone may have waited for me.

My first days paring sticks into piles of curled scraps were nothing more than a way to exhaust those days, to hope that when I next lifted my head the sun would have abandoned another afternoon. And even if I am now more practiced at such distraction, those first years' birds would never fly—wings lopsided, tails stunted, no feathers for the wind to ruffle. If I have kept any from those days it is only to remind myself of what I have since learned; if I have taken money for my birds it is only that a man who cannot raise his own foods still must eat. Now I have idled here seaside long enough, and tonight I will put away my tools; study not the shore lights, but the map my wife hung on the wall long ago.

When Bill Quincy next comes, I will give back to him the faded and folded bills he has given me over the years. I will ask him to bring me an axe. For that water was no waste: stunted by years of wind, the pines have grown tough, crooked and knotted, too stout for the saws I keep oiled in the shed. I can stay no longer, I will tell him, because even after the trees are felled that twisted wood will take weeks to cut and plane, to smooth and fit into the planks to build my boat—on such a passage I can no longer trust my dinghy, ignorant of waves these seven years. And the day I launch my boat into the weave of waves and unfurl my sackcloth sail will be only the beginning—then I must follow the birds as they usher me to the edge of land, miles and miles of unknown country ranging west, ocean-vast; the currents of roads, the swells of hills and hollows, the flow of fields washing me at last to the home where my wife and child wait.

# SIGNS

The signs the County installed for that Peck boy got
tore down just a week after they went up. Not long
after the Pecks moved into the old Marshall place, men
in one of those green County trucks pulled onto the
shoulder of our road. They dug round holes and planted
each sign a quarter mile from the Peck house, facing
opposite ways. Didn't take more than an hour. They stood
there smoking, looking out over my fields and Peck's
unplowed land. Their two signs threw tiny diamonds of
shadow on the ground. Then they left.

After they'd gone, I noticed the Peck boy, dirty-faced
and lying in the shade of some overgrown lilacs—watching all along everything they'd been doing, I imagined.
That was when I realized he lay there most days, studying

me up on my porch. Since the gout came bad, sitting was about all I could take. We lived just across the way from the Pecks.

Mr. Peck said he figured it was the same kids who'd dented his mailbox with rocks earlier in the summer who tore down the signs. Even the posts had been taken down. Two patches of loose earth were all to show where they'd stood. Next day, Mr. Peck stood by the road holding a stopwatch as the cars came barreling down it. Dust clouded the air after they passed.

"It's flat," I told him, "straight as an arrow."

He said he didn't care. "Fifty-five miles an hour," he said. "Sixty, some of them." He sent off a letter to the County.

Course no one would have blamed any kid who'd done it. That Peck boy once took it upon himself to lead the singing at Sunday service, standing up and swaying like some wild animal in the middle of sermon. His father had to drag him out by the hand, and the whole time that boy's mouth just a round wet yelping thing. Sometimes at night I heard him from across the road. In our forty-seven years here, we'd never once locked the door before they moved in. Ellen lost her sleep, kept up nights with nerves.

We didn't much take to special rights, or whatever the County would claim. We knew who was paying for those signs, and who was paying for the special teacher who knew how to talk with her hands. Some said the Peck boy was simple, but I saw his eyes staring at me and simple wasn't what I cared to call it. He knew exactly what he was up to.

The son-in-law came by to plow under the old corn the same day the new signs went up. From the porch

I watched those men in their green uniforms digging holes again. Their feet kicked up dust the wind took with it. Out on the fields Ron drove my Massey-Ferguson in circles. Stalks twisted and went down. Ellen carried a glass of tea out to me and said, "What a shame."

It was a few weeks later Mr. Peck found the two missing signs, the first ones. Indian summer, a bright October afternoon with the sky a dusty blue. Birds circled over spent fields, gathering on wires for the flight south. We'd been up to Cournoyer's that morning and bought some pumpkins, and Ellen was setting them on the porch steps. I was sitting out back like I'd come to do recently, out of sight of the Peck place. Then Ellen came rushing around the corner of the house. "I can't stand it anymore," she said. "I can't stand it."

I limped out front. Across the way I saw the two yellow signs lying in the dry grass of the Pecks' yard from wherever Mr. Peck had dragged them out. The other two signs still stood, looking away from what was happening. Mr. Peck bent over the ones in the grass, and that boy lay in the grass too, sprawled at his father's feet. In his hand Mr. Peck swung his belt. His voice carried across the road, echoing off the front of our house and vanishing into the fields.

My arms hung at my sides. That boy didn't make a sound. Even his hands just scrabbled at the dirt as he tried to squirm out of his father's reach.

All those birds dipped and spun, their feathers black against the burnt grass.

# DEAR OKLAHOMA

Oh, Oklahoma, I have looked for you in so many
places, hunted everywhere I thought would yield
a brief glimpse of you, driven so many miles along roads
unnamed and untraveled, roads I hoped would lead me
to you. In a stubbled cornfield pale with March frost,
in a line of sagging clothes stretched beside a bowed
barn, in the curve of a woman's back as she bent to lift
her child—there I believed I saw you. My uncle, at seventeen, hitchhiked from Forge Village, Massachusetts,
into your heart before he lost his way beside a church's
vacant doors, the bell in its steeple dark and silent, and
turned back toward us again. A child of that same state, I
too thought of you, of that emptiness the tales about you
told, the skies above you as broad as the blanket that each

night smothered me. Oklahoma, it was myself I thought you would save me from, taking me traceless into you, your rumpled lap a comfort to these bones accustomed to unforgiving granite. And Graniteville Road—the road where my uncle spent the afternoons of his own boyhood, the road where, having seen you once, he thought his feet would lead him. But I am not so fickle, Oklahoma; I am ready to give myself up to you, to take your outstretched arm and swing myself toward you.

Oklahoma, Oklahoma, even your name possesses me, the home I see at your end. For years I have called you as if my voice could shape your body. Once I thought I saw you in western New York, in the peeled paint of a collapsing farmhouse perched over a shadowed valley, in the limitless roll of bluelined clouds, in a halo of crows inscribing itself on a winter's dusk, in a junked car of delicate rust, black-eyed Susans blooming from the crevices of its hood. On South Carolina's roads of red dirt I thought of you. In the cant of telephone poles and wind-swaying wires, in the dusty words of a book long unopened, you were close. For years now you have not left me—even when, for a time, I have forgotten you.

A woman I once knew, a woman who had grown up beside your borders, her hair the gold-spun flax of a bedtime story, told me that, among those hills I called my own, outside felt to her like inside; that even our skies pressed upon her. We have all felt that, I answered her. And we have. In our state, the lichen-spotted trunks of trees spread branches to catch anything rising up; the land folds in on itself to harbor secrets; the weather is alchemy. Our nights break with unhurried assurance; days, the shadows everything casts move across our uneven soil like nets. The clouds trail strings of rain, the seas swallow our coasts, the clapboards we nail to our houses weep water. Ghosts collect in our hollows and along our riverbanks, then rise as fog on moonless nights. The wind blows tales of the dead; our forebears speak in the creak and settle of our homes. The only fires we know we confine in blackened iron, in sooty brick, where we can feed them chunks of wood and the scraps of our living, and there we marshal ourselves to hoard that warmth, to remember what was and, as we voice it, still is. No one is unbound, and while our weather happens to us we invent places of sunlight and space, places we name for you, Oklahoma, places where anyone may vow to forget, and, in forgetting, become himself.

Nights, this woman lit yellow lamps in every room of her house, a fire on her hearth and candles on her table. She spread her hair on the pillow and read to me, stories of a man who left his home for a map's blank space, where he built another; stories of a man who returned to look in his own window years and years later at the woman he scarcely recognized. Why did you leave, I asked her, and, Will you return to yours someday? And as she spoke I took that wheat-colored hair in my hands, slippery and elusive as it parted around my fingers and fell to the pillow—thinking of you, Oklahoma; thinking of my uncle and the two fists of you he held before he turned his back to you for what he knew already.

The woman sang to me your song as she drove me, plumbing the wishes of lapsed towns, weedy orchards red with the memory of apples, our abandoned country of fallen fences, morning rides I peered through streaked glass for your face looking back at me, the face I knew I would recognize because it would remind me so much of my own. You are the land and the land belongs to

us. But the words of the song she taught me those days
have faded. She notched a cigarette between two fingers,
its end burning toward her knuckles as we meandered
along roads winding to the shapes of our hills, roads
shadowed by the boughs of dark trees, roads doubling
back on themselves, uncertain of where they would lead,
so that the woman, as she drove, turned the steering
wheel's knobbed curve around and around in her hands.
I will show you Oklahoma, she said.

Oklahoma, what she showed me were things I had
never known: pressing my head against her chest to hear
the roaming currents of blood inside; swishing the ends
of her hair, July bright, across my back while I stretched
on my stomach, forehead to clasped hands. All of the
yellow lights she had touched into being—switch, wick,
kindling—flickered all around us, moving over us as we
moved in her house, and for a time, I confess, I did not
think of my uncle, did not think of you. Here, she said,
taking my hand in hers; here, and here. My mouth on
her skin I did not imagine the sweet tang of your red
dust rising to chalk my tongue. This is Oklahoma, she
said, here.

But, Oklahoma, you are the heart of things—the
dirt ringing your ankles, the sweat on your neck, the
waterless seasons of your eyes. I have come to understand
this, if slowly. All roads lead to where you are, center of
the body's arterial map. You escape photographs; and
even these words, I know, will never find you. On your
body, every line is only someone's dream, a possibility
traced across your skin, disappearing as a finger is lifted.
Did my uncle foresee, I wonder, as he walked west the
length of this state, turning at the glow of headlights to
raise his hand, that he would travel, finally, to you? He

may never have imagined you, as he lay one night in a briared culvert and watched nameless stars circle him, nor as he swung himself into the heated cab of a truck where a man eyed the frayed cuffs of his jeans, his lashes clumped with rain: the three-day smell of him, his breath steaming the window he leaned against while he asked the man could he smoke, while wipers scraped twin swathes of vision. Oklahoma, when I one day find you I will ask you these questions. I will hope that you can give me answers, even if your answers are lies. For I can only imagine my uncle—seventeen, and me, his sister's son, already a child asleep somewhere among hills lost in the bellies of clouds—as he climbed down from the truck to the blacktop's sheen, then pocketed his hands and turned to you for the first time: no mirage, the flicker and sway of that landscape he faced. He headed off to the bridge he saw before him, where the waters slurring around the pilings below washed red mud—across it, and then, so easily, he had found you—the low fields where weather is born, the tin-roofed houses of your family, the people who with their words would have welcomed him if the skeletal wind had not filled his ears with its rushing, erasing the sound of their speech.

Did he sleep in your soft arms, Oklahoma, as you smoothed the dirty hair from his forehead and beneath his lids his dark eyes fluttered, or did he, wide awake, burrow straight through the heat and blown dust to your heart, his own restless blood trembling in his neck? For four nights my grandmother did not sleep, she said later, until at dawn a silver coin dropped into a slot hundreds of miles away sent his voice to hers through those wires that have always reminded me of you. He was coming home, he said, staring up through the booth's glass at the steeple of a church, evening roost of birds who scatter days to gather bugs and bits of string. And then, the answer to a question, he spoke your name—the open space at its beginning, its end reminding him of what waited for him. When he hung the phone in its cradle, my grandmother fell asleep at last, she told me, and slept a night, a day, another night.

When the woman told me stories, those nights in her house, I was silent, and she thought that I had no stories to tell her, no songs, that my voice was caught within these crooked hills. But I imagined my uncle embracing you, clutching you with both hands, and words would not come, Oklahoma. I saw him, opening the hinged glass door, and stepping into your wide belt, all of you I had never seen—a country my mind, narrow as these valleys, could never imagine. He may have had no more coins in his pocket; he may have lied to his mother. He may still sleep curled within you, bed a raft on your still waters. For years his ageless face watched me when I visited Graniteville Road—here, in white light, a summer day, he leaned over a garden spade; here he squatted beside a rocky stream and, smiling, held a trout in his hands as if it were a gift. Oklahoma, can an image invoke a person any more than a map does a place? Is it enough for me to say that I cannot hear his voice, that the stories I know about him first cluttered the memories of others? My uncle has been the man we saw stepping from the bank, who vanished in the time we drove around the block, the man we imagined tapping on our door the middle of some night, the boy we saw posed on Route 225's edge, late, hair in his face as he aimed his thumb at our low sky. For years when the phone rang we believed we would hear his voice, and sometimes we let it ring unanswered: we have been disappointed so many times.

One night, I waited for the woman to hold back her hair with one hand as she leaned to breathe the candles into smoke; as she let the fire's embers fail, and turned off the lamps. Rain crackled from the eaves. In bed already, I heard her draw her dress over her hair's swishing fall, felt the room's cool air slip in with her as she bared the mattress and let the covers settle across us. If she spoke, all I heard was wind whisking the roof, rain streaming down the windows. And I remembered you, your warm skin wavering before me, your gentle swells, your rippled fields and pearl skies, all your country I longed to see. In that house's dark, I knew she could not help me find you. For so long living near you she had forgotten what you were; showing me herself she had shown me only you. Even now, when I try to recall her face, her voice, her name, all I see is this place I have come to. Her hair, that night, spread itself on the pillow, pooled in a shoulder's hollow. I raked my fingers through it, and when she stirred, one hand sweeping beneath the sheet to clutch a knot of blanket, I let my feet lead me to you, west over streams and rivers; into the mountains where I saw you at the horizon's blurred line; and down into this wide bowl whose bottom you are.

It is late now, Oklahoma, and I have no one to say these words to but you. Listen when I call your name, its syllables a song in themselves; let your fierce winds carry it to your ends.

I will raise a house with my own hands, here in your fields where all maps fail me, and when you come, Oklahoma, I will welcome you—at last, at last.

# SUNDOWNING

At sundown it is the dog in the ice, the dog barking upriver in the dark, the bare trees coated with sleet, the snow crusted with more ice, the doorknob she wraps her hands around, tugging.

This is what she has told me.

A child, I spoke of what had been hidden, that part of her grandfather hid before he left. How else to speak of it? We—a sister, a brother—watched her walk through the house, out into the yard, staring and muttering at the grass around her ankles. "Henry," we heard her say, "Henry," over and over, and we said she was looking for him to get back that part of herself he had taken away.

We said the part of her that remembered names to things.

She is at the door, her fingers finding the cracks around it and slipping in until I take them and hold them in my own, before the nails can tear, the tips become bloody. Such has happened.

She sits by the window and watches. At a foot kicking a leaf or tires hissing over wet pavement she raises her head, speaks of a man and a farm and a barn full of cows, horses loose in the fields, pie cooling on the counter.

"Henry," she says, "where are you hiding? Why do you hide from me?"

Those days, as the quiet grew hour by hour until the wind came back to blow it away, nothing had only one name. "Helen," she called sister, and "Yes?" she, sister, said.

"I just saw a wolf atop Ben Young Hill," she says.

This dog I cannot figure, this dog barking and barking.

Her eyes invisible behind glasses reflecting circles of hard light.

There is a place I don't know the name of, a name I have heard but cannot say, a name I once knew but forgot, a wrong name someone told me, a name I have never pronounced correctly, a name that has since been changed to another name. It is a name that means nothing but a place. Or it is a name named for the man who found it.

We speak, or else don't. "He walked off under that tree and left me," she says, and that is that.

Those days, in the dark room, I told her, sister, that by evening she looked hardest for that part of herself we knew was missing—buried in the loose dirt grandfather had worked, or stuck in the crook of an old tree, higher than anyone but grandfather could have reached.

She, years before even this, would promise a quarter for her earring or the keys to the car long since become grass-grown rust in a field, bricks against rotted tires. We would search below the skirts of her chairs, hunt through crabgrass, peer into dark cellar corners where cucumbers set to pickle and jars of applesauce and blackberry jam gathered dust, thick and waxy. Sacks of potatoes grew eyes as long as our fingers, and these we did not disturb.

We traced and retraced her steps.

We walk up the street, she leaning against me, burying her head in my chest as cars pass. Boots, cuffs flecked with wet gravel and mud. "Where has the river gone, did it dry up too?"

A place, yes, where men flooded the river, where over years the water rose over roofs—but that is not where she names.

Now I hunt up the spaces between things, that place and some memory, what she says.

Each morning we sit side by side, passing the pictures between us, spreading them on our knees, her fingers hooking them and bringing them to her nose: an exercise I am supposed to encourage. "Oh, yes," she says. "I know that man. The jars in his pantry were filled with bugs."

It was she, sister, who decided she would stay with me.

By the window, we listen for the dog as the room turns dark. I say nothing. "Hush!" she says.

The house shakes when trucks pass. Lamps rattle, and a picture once fell from the wall.

She rests her hand against the pane.

I listened by the crack of her door for her slow wheeze, then went out into the night, shimmying trees, overturning rocks, licking away the spiderwebs that stuck to my lips and wiping them from my eyelashes as I hunted what was lost in the dark, those nights, the threads trailing behind me.

In the woods the dog circles a tree, barking, and she pushes aside branches.

Air slides under the ice, green bubbles; her feet punch holes in the snow's pebbled crust. To imagine breaking through from below: she walks through the woods.

Or she is walking, circling the floor, her feet trying to wear through the boards to some hidden place underneath, knocking papers from a table, overturning a plant, bunching the rug, until I come.

"I have to get them horses into the barn," she tells me.

"Alfred," she says, hand to my cheek. "Jake, I say. Charlie."

"Henry."

Those days, from the top of a tree, I watched one afternoon become evening as the sun sank behind the ridge, a fire in the spaces between trees fading as the house fell under growing shadow, the windows darkening or else glowing with lamplight, so that when I turned only the last bit of it was left to wink out.

# THE DEAD MAN

Spiders web our corners, stitch threads across doorways we break passing through. Mice burrow into soil hardening each day, squeeze through the cracked foundation, and scuttle under the silent radiators, scratching inside the walls in the dark—"Nesting," Junie says. At night we hear birds settle in the eaves. Dust billows in streamers from the ceiling. Dangles and swings. Quarters, dimes, nickels—no pennies, only silver—fill rust-edged coffee cans. Junie makes a fire of twigs and rolled newspaper and we boil a pot of water for tea, sweeping the still-hot ash out the front door as soon as the water steams. On the plank floor a blackening circle grows daily.

We sleep on the plank floor, knocking ankles and knees when we turn over, breathing the dust from the cracks between boards. We roll, tangle; stretch and settle. We are our warmth. The blankets that we have we pile on top of us, where they pool and wrinkle, bunch, in the trough between us. We light candles in the dark, sticking them one by one on the old nails we've banged through shingles pulled from the outside of the house. Windows rattle loose and small flames flutter—Junie sold the curtains, or used them to patch ripped knees. Our breath floats free over the blankets.

"It will be a train," Junie says, "and a countryside too dark to see. How can you leave a place but by the same way you arrived?"

At night, when Junie talks, her words hang in the dark above us for a moment before they, too, float away.

Junie wears the dead man's boots—how small he was, this dead man—small enough that even Junie must tug the boots on, stomping her heels into place. "Do you think it will give any, this leather?" Junie asks, lacing the laces into the dark grooves they've carved across the tongue.

"This dead man has walked all over this country," Junie says, climbing a hill or cutting across a field to the bluff where the river loops and we watch all that water churning south.

We've kept pillows, and the clothes we've worn all season, a can opener and dishes, one place serving each, boxes of colored candles, wooden kitchen matches that splinter our fingers lighting wicks. I keep my rabbit's foot pocketed, touching those blunted nails and the tufted hair between them when Junie puffs out our lights with a breath. Pots and pans hold frost-cold water, slushy some mornings, edges ice-stitched. An old suitcase belted shut holds everything else: Junie's rubber-banded photographs, needles slid through spools of thread, the buck knife Junie said she will use to skin anyone who gives us trouble.

"When we leave we will leave all this," Junie says. "Nothing we can't carry ourselves."

What else there was we sold, Junie in the truck driving to pawn her rings and earrings though not, she said, ever the necklace I had once given her in a tissued box. Then when the tall man had handed to Junie a stack of bills and driven off in the truck it was the other men who came in other trucks with dollies and leather gloves and loud boots, lifting out the table and chairs, the couch and scuffed dressers, the beds—theirs, big, the men tilted sideways to fit through the doorway; mine one man hefted to a shoulder while he walked to the truck—and lastly the stove and refrigerator. Soon the men, all of them, were gone. Soon it was what Junie called knickknacks and leftovers on a fold-out card table in the front yard. Old women stopped their cars on the way home from services and lifted tumblers to the sun to check for hairlines, overturned the salt and pepper shakers, examined the frayed cord of the iron, slid their arms into the sleeves of Junie's sweaters. Their husbands lifted the lid of the rattly box of mostly rusty tools Junie said was all he'd left us, when he left; they poked through nails and washers and paint-handled screwdrivers and the blunted saw before letting the lid fall shut again. My job was watching hands and pockets; Junie counted out coins, plucked a fluttering bill from someone's fingers. What was unclaimed after a week I brought to town to carry door to door, ringing bells and holding up peelers and pencil cases, coloring books only three pages used, the paperback mysteries Junie said she'd read one after the next those months she was big with me, lace doilies from a dresser drawer. Hands turned back the edges of curtains and faces looked at me, there, a cardboard box of all these things held before me.

"What do we need beyond a blanket to roll around ourselves?" Junie asks. "Far to the south, at night, at any time of year, we can lie in palmetto grass—and there, we won't need even that blanket. A gulf's curve of lowlands where the trees and hillsides won't block our view."

After our tea we step to the yard, the grass that went to seed in summer now pale and brittle, the ends frayed but still taller than my waist. "Can you smell it?" Junie asks, and on the wind I smell woodsmoke, the wet bark of trees, and a smell I think smells like the cool barrel of the gun Junie kept in the closet until the end of summer, when another man came to the house, peered its length, and gave to Junie more bills, a clump of them he carefully unfolded and smoothed out on the leg of his jeans.

"I came through the hills, along the river, looking through the window of a train," Junie says. "North. It was night and my own face looked back at me. Do you think I saw where I had come to before I stepped down from the car, to where he stood waiting for me on the platform? Do you think I would still have come?"

Of him there was usually so little that now, remembering, mostly what I remember is nothing except him being somewhere not there, or asking Junie where he was, or waking under a blanket's spill over me on the couch, the television a field of flickering snow, to see her at the dark window, breath a blur on glass.

"What use is there in remembering him?" Junie says, if I ask. "You're the one good thing he ever gave me."

On nights the sky is cast over with clouds there is no

light but the stutter of our candles. Wax drips, puddles, dries: red and white beads on the floor I scrape with a fingernail. On the wall our shadows shiver and jump.

"What is a pillow," Junie says, "but a place to hold the sad shapes our head makes while we sleep? Is that comfort?"

We wake to geese at night, the faint sound of their passing drifting down to us from skies too dark to see them in. Their sleepy bleat a lullaby like the rain that freezes as it hits the window, a clock's click and whirr of toothed gears, though Junie and I no longer know any hour.

There is always something to wake us.

A train's long whistle through the hills will keep us up half the night.

Each night we wait for the snow, for that snow we can feel already in the air, for the tick of rain and sleet to change to a sound we can no longer hear.

In the mornings frost whitens hollows in the grass. The man from the bank comes to look at the sign he pounded into near-frozen earth two weeks ago, the wood stake gray and splintery. Heads just below the windowsill, we can hear his car pull off the gravel road, hear the thump as his door swings shut, hear the swish of dry grass against his pants.

The man from the bank calls out to us, saying what he has said already so many times about papers and properties and about how what he wants, least of all, he always says, is any kind of trouble. Junie says that he cannot see us and does not know where we lie hidden. "He isn't even sure he's not talking to himself," Junie says.

The man from the bank shades a hand over his eyes to look.

"Never," Junie says, "listen to what a man says when there's something of yours he is after."

The man from the bank never stays long. We watch him, this slouching man trying to fill his suits. We watch him circle the house, lifting his feet high as he steps through the grass, and clutching to his chest always a supply of papers, or a clipboard of fluttering papers, or a briefcase which must, Junie and I imagine, hold papers and more papers, stacks of papers. We watch him approach the door, lift two knuckles to the wood, and squint through a dusty window; we watch him tuck those papers up under his arm and turn to leave. We watch as he eases himself back into his car to back it over bending grass, as its white smoke rises in the cold air, as its lights blink red for a moment before he drives the car away.

And then we are walking, Junie and I, walking always to our bluff, Junie walking the dead man's boots to places, she says, she doesn't know if the dead man has ever been, or else to places, she says, that his boots may know well—across ground as familiar as the feel of the dead man's foot once was. It was the dead man's heart that failed him, a little heart that Junie says must have had to beat harder and faster as the dead man climbed these hills that ring us, these hills that before long we must always climb to some hilltop or another, where, if there are no trees, we can see only hills and more hills; where the clouds are low enough to touch. But when his heart failed him his boots were still not old, the heels not worn down, the leather still glossy with the dead man's polish—not old enough to throw out with the rest of the dead man's things, the dead man's widow told the woman at the church sale, who gave the boots to Junie in a paper bag crumpled and curled over at the top.

At the bluff the trees lean out over the river and from one, Junie says, her hand against it and bits of its loose bark floating down to the water, it would be an easy drop, a matter of feet, at worst a bump and a bruise. The river curves against the hill and currents cross; a stick dropped in here spins and spins before the river takes it to the places Junie tells of—or not even that far, since it is not the river we will follow to those places but the train tracks that here follow the river, trace the curve of hill and water, the twin rails rusty along their sides but polished to a dull sheen on top. Each evening the train comes, metal wheels against metal rails as the train snakes along the valley, the train men braking the train to keep it, here, from falling into the river. Below us, it moves no faster than we, on top of the bluff, could walk beside it.

The wind, sometimes, carries with it the smell of the paper mill downriver, the brick buildings where huge bundles of paper sit on loading docks, where the foaming waters turn different colors some days, where smoke rises straight into the low clouds and just makes them darker. Before the tall man drove away in Junie's truck, we, driving past the mill, would see men clustered on those loading docks, holding cigarettes by their hips, lifting a thermos of coffee, staring out into the rain at the cars splashing by. Their hands, we knew, carried the stink of pulp and dye. And with the scrape of wipers over glass, Junie would say, looking at me looking, "Don't bother, he isn't there." Now, sniffing the air, Junie crooks her elbow over her nose and mouth, and when she talks like that the words come muffled from her sleeve. "It was a good trick," Junie says, "he played, bringing me here. He told me of fall's red leaves, winter moons, trees shining silver in afternoon light. A house with a view of the hills, a bed he'd build for us himself beside a wide window. How pretty it will all be, I thought, and the train windows showed me only my own mute face."

All around us the curled shapes of leaves still stuck to bare branches rattle in the wind.

"This," Junie says, looking at her feet, "is the best kind of man to have."

"Any man's heart may fail him," Junie says.

These days the dark gathers the bare trees and hills and empty roads into itself so quickly, and sometimes by the time we are headed back we are heading through branches we can no longer see before us, along a road we cannot tell where it leads until a car crests a hill or rounds a curve and catches us in its lights. Then Junie parts the grass before our dark house, walks to the door, while I untangle a sleeve from a clump of burrs, yank a cuff caught on barbed wire.

"We will wait for the snow," Junie says. "The snow will be our sign."

"Do you think the dead man was an old man first?" she asks.

"We'll pack," Junie says, "our things into bundles, drape the blankets around ourselves, and drop down. Have you ever seen a train take a mail bag?" she asks. "Do you know how much ground a train can cross while everyone else in the world sleeps?"

We eat crackers from the boxes and boxes of them Junie bought in town the day before the tall man came to give her the money for the truck, crackers with apples we take from the heap of them in the corner of the room we called the kitchen—apples we, weeks back, gathered and heaped there from the orchards that grow up all over this country. Junie, making tea, leans into the kettle's plume of steam; rubs her hands together in those vanishing clouds.

"Just think," Junie says, "how we'll take the dead man away from these hills, too. But when we get to the place where the grass grows thick all year, where the air smells of oranges and salt, where no hills block our view, where the only winds are warm, then we won't need boots anymore."

"Where will we leave the dead man, then?" I ask Junie.

"We'll leave him on the train," Junie says, "in the car that carries us those nights, in the car that, when we jump from it, will continue on its way wherever the rails lead it."

Junie blows out the candle.

We wrap the blankets around us, hearing as we do the geese flying through the night, and, rolling to one side and then another, knock the plank floor with our ankles, our elbows, our knees.

This is all there is to it.

In my pocket, my hand strokes the fur of my rabbit's foot.

We dream snow.

I try to imagine our house, then—grass poking up through the snow or else bent and buried beneath it, snow covering the roof, snow thick on the stairs when the man from the bank comes, carrying papers, to call out to us from the driveway and then, squinting his eyes against all that whiteness, to walk to our door where, waiting, he will tap his knuckles twice.

And in that snow, that first snow—flakes braiding down around us, every branch and bush outlined in white, the train men peering through it to slow for the curve where river and tracks loop to the south and the bluff rises against pale clouds—in that snow, when we have gone, anyone may come to one of these sparse fields, one of these stretches of bare trees where snow covers gray grass and old leaves, where the pulp's sour reek hangs in the air, and follow the tracks of the dead man's boots to see the way we got away—but hurry: already the footsteps fill with what is still falling.